Tears of the Weaver

Tears *of the* Weaver

Zaheera Jina Asvat

modjaji books

Published in 2023 by Modjaji Books
Cape Town, South Africa
© Zaheera Jina Asvat

www.modjajibooks.co.za

ISBN 978-1-991240-00-2 (print)
ISBN 978-1-991240-01-9 (e-book)

Editor: Nerine Dorman
Proofreader: Sue Carver
Cover artwork and lettering: Jesse Breytenbach
Cover, book and text design and layout: Liz Gowans
Set in Constantia 10/12 pt.

Dedication

For the people who reside within communities like Lenasia...

Contents

Foreword

"like all hand-woven tapestries, this one, too, held the tears of its weaver. It held mother's tears. And it was strategically placed to hide the scarred wall that wore signs of a battle once fought. That tapestry was almost perfect, while our lives wore the rot of a waning reality."
(The Tears of the Weaver)

A product of Apartheid's Group Areas Act, Lenasia became home for South African Indians who were forced out of interracial areas across Johannesburg. Geographically displaced and politically discouraged from engaging with the world beyond their borders, Lenasians slowly fell into the mundane rhythm of a community. It was not difficult for a shared sense of 'Indianness' to reverberate through this echo chamber, and people soon revisited ideas from the old continent about who is a neighbour, a friend, and who is not – even though many an ancestor might have fled from these very descriptions. Nevertheless, it lulled the community into a false sense of safety, and seeing themselves as separated and separate from others, Lenasians, for the most part, sought to protect the fragile socio-economic privilege that Apartheid had meted out to them. Viewed from this perspective, it is possible to say that Apartheid urban planning was a raging success, for it allowed people to spin a palace out of a jail. Today, Lenasia has gone through many moultings, yet its insidious inception continues to play out in the lives of its people.

Zaheera Jina Asvat's short stories serve as a window into this world. They are not nostalgic accounts of kinship and community, but a rather brazen, unflinching gaze at those who struggle against the confines of 'Lenasian identity'. These stories capture the domestic rhythms and social patterns of contemporary Lenasia and use this rich tapestry to mark the experiences of characters who cannot knit themselves into this social fabric. Whether they be a foreigner, a child, a housewife or a mother, each story encompasses a wilful spirit who is seeking to peer beyond the veil of the status quo to reach for something new or different. Yet Jina Asvat shows through the sharply drawn characters that the yearning to 'go beyond' is far from romantic. Our dreams – both big and small – always come at the cost of our communal comfort. As characters realise that they have been lulled by social norms, the narrative voice does not step in to allay the fear and anxiety that comes with dropping the role in which they have been cast. We are expected to carry the pain of the characters, such that we also imbibe the existential quest of what it means to be alive on our own terms.

Jina Asvat's style is a departure from the sentimentalised, melodramatic tones that are often used to represent Indians, and by extension, South African Indians. Instead, Jina Asvat's bare prose reveals lapses in the South African Indian lexicon that cannot articulate various forms of psychological and emotional distress. For fear of ruining the tapestry, characters are caught in waves of private pain and yearning that mutate and leak into other forms of oblique expression. Yet, because these communicative gaps are also calls to weave words out of their tears, the challenge of enlisting the necessary courage and language to articulate personal difference is also one that belongs to the reader, and so these characters lay bare a fundamentally human experience in a way that carries us from Lenasia to the world.

Dr Nedine Moonsamy *(The Unfamous Five)*
13th April 2020
Johannesburg

Bewitched

'The early morning walk was beautiful today, my love,' says Mr Asmal. 'It is always that way because Allah has blessed me with legs to walk.'

He praises Allah often, sometimes during the day, but mostly in prayer. As a result, he carries his wooden-beaded tasbeeh around all the time, especially these days when uncertainty has returned to their abode. There is so little happiness left here that it needs to be nurtured to life like a delicate white orchid – through an abundance of patience, praise, and prayer.

Mr Asmal is different from his wife, for she has become so dismal that she forgets to thank Allah for the small mercies. She spends hours in a day lamenting past injustices and what could have been. She also laments her daughter being doomed a spinster, but her worries in this regard are often whispered in hushed tones through heaving sobs.

Mr Asmal does not waste his life in worry. He has long accepted their sealed fate. It is cast in stone. During the early days, they bore the curse in disbelief – it would never happen. However, they still held faith through sixteen years of happiness, believing that their daughter would marry until that day when karma became a bitch.

But the reality of the foreboding curse has come, between their avenged past and this new present. The past mocks them, often like a nightmare. But now, even the harsh reality of the present has passed. This is a new future, and it must be mourned. Mr Asmal forgets to mourn – he is thankful for life's small mercies.

Mrs Asmal is beyond annoyed by his nonchalance. Whenever he utters one of his praises, she screams, 'Oh please be quiet!'

She has begun to loathe him, her hatred naked to the sun. People say that they need grandchildren to mend their split hearts. If only their only child has not been destined to remain an old maid.

Muslim custom is that men walk in front and women follow, but Mrs Asmal rushes ahead of Mr Asmal, who often stops to marvel at the creation of most things. It is a painful sight, these days, to see them together in social spaces. He, short and stout, with a rounded belly (which he is always thankful for), and she, tall and thin with a milky white face pleated with wrinkles. Sometimes they are seen with her aggressively pulling him along, like one would a mooing cow. This is an accepted sight of a discontented marriage, to their daughter Fa'eeza Asmal, who sees marriage only as a means of procreation. She does not know the romantic tragedy of their love, for it has to be kept a secret from her.

'I feel the tears of sadness wanting to spill from these eyes, which Allah has so generously blessed me with,' says Mr Asmal.

'Voetsek, man!' Blobs of spit escape from Mrs Asmal's usually pursed lips.

More tragedy has fallen on them. They have just received the devastating news that Fa'eeza Asmal, their beloved and only child, has yet again been rejected by an eligible suitor. She now, at the ripe age of thirty-one, remains a spinster.

Fa'eeza is not called Fa'eeza. People use both her name and surname when they talk about her, because of her being recognised as an omen child, so to speak. Everybody knows of her notorious fairy-tale birth.

***

Once upon a time, a beautiful baby girl named Khadija was born. Her skin was as white as milk, and her lips were a rosy red. Her hair grew golden in shimmering locks down her back. From the tender age of only four, her mother would comb her hair, sitting on the balcony beneath the twilight moon, heedless of those who watched. Baal, the jinn who was naughty, playful, and promiscuous, eyed the fair maiden from his place hidden in the dense forest beyond their home. And, as the years melted, and he saw less of her – and even though he only heard the happiness in her laugh, or caught a glimpse of the shimmer of her hair as it brushed her growing breasts – the more he sought and desired her. And upon that seeded moment, on her sixteenth birthday, in the wake of her monthly bleeding – he claimed her. He watched her hair dance in soft curls to the fattened white moon and then, with greedy eyes, he reached out and bewitched her with treacherous obsession.

It is said that when Baal's fingers touched her hair, his spirit passed through Khadija and escaped from her in the form of a blaze of lightning. Khadija fell to the ground, and for three days she remained unconscious. When she came to, she no longer spoke, though she laughed or cried often. Some say that the shock of a bad jinn passing through her form had driven her mad, but others claim that the light in her eyes was one of tranquillity. Be that as it may, from that moment, until years later, Khadija's hair fell off in locks, leaving her hairless. She sat on the balcony for days without moving, staring at her reflection in her vanity mirror. If her mother brought her food, she sometimes ate, but often she left it untouched.

Mr Asmal came – some say it was a few weeks later, some say it was years – the paak jinn had summoned him to release her – Khadija the captured heroine.

He was so determined and courageous, our hero who held the power of prayer, that he conquered Baal in a vicious carnage of magic and resilient prayer. Baal retreated to the blackened abyss of doom, but before accepting defeat, he cursed the boy child who came from Khadija's womb.

With his departure, a blackened sense of foreboding seeped into crevices within the house, drowning it in trepidation. Outside, a muted decay emerged on the house's walls from under the paint. Creepers shuttered windows and barricaded the house into an enraged cage. Trapped inside, they all awaited tragedy.

And it came: it came at the crack of dawn when the serpentine branches of trees tapped an eerie tone of mourning on the windowpanes – that was when, with trembling hands, she tore the lifeless corpse from inside her. It returned with the shrill tone of a ravenous bird in anticipation of the bloodied remnants. It came five times and stole all of them – five baby boys, dead. And after the death of their fifth prince, Khadija accepted defeat.

But He is the planner – Allah the Lord of the worlds.

And, ultimately, with the commitment of their love and with Allah's infinite power, Mr Asmal and Khadija gave birth to a healthy baby girl whom they named Fa'eeza. Victorious, winner, successful.

They kept her captive until the morning of her sixteenth birthday.

That morning, the house had opened its dusty eyelids, intrigued by the tainted innocence of young Fa'eeza Asmal and the comfort of her happiness at finally being released into the outside world. Fa'eeza Asmal was now ready to become betrothed. People came from far and wide with their sons to meet her; some contrived sons only so that they could get a glimpse of the protected girl.

'They do not accept her,' grumbled Khadija.

'They will. It is still early days, my love,' Mr Asmal consoled his wife. 'She is Fa'eeza, our victorious princess.'

'They will say that she, too, is possessed. Remember Banoo's son, Ishmael? He really liked Fa'eeza, he wanted to make nikaah with her the moment that he saw her, and then, Banoo never called.'

'Yes, Khadija, but did you really want Ishmael as a son-in-law? He has rotten teeth! Our daughter can't marry the likes of him!'

'It worries me. Do you think that our daughter has been cursed? Maybe we should take her to a maulana...'

'Khadija, we are not taking Fa'eeza to a maulana. Word will spread, and they will really think that something is wrong with her. If they do not accept her, so be it. Allah knows best!' exclaimed Mr Asmal.

***

It had come back to the day when Mr Asmal had forbidden Khadija from going to the maulana. He had deemed it unnecessary.

The early evidence of this rejection had happened a good fifteen years before when Fa'eeza Asmal had turned sixteen and was pronounced of age to wed. The Asmals had become the talk of Lenasia because of their notorious fairy-tale past. Nobody else had such an extraordinary past, and to Khadija's pride and happiness, her daughter had survived a good many years, and so she was delighted to crack open the chrysalis and watch her only daughter emerge like a butterfly into the wide-open world.

But the panchat aunties of Lenasia had to burst Khadija's bubble by spreading rumours of Fa'eeza Asmal's strange past and 'giant-like' features. Anything for a good gossip story.

These happenings consume Khadija. Mr Asmal refuses to allow her space to lament. He turns his back on her tears, and so through the years, their love that they once fought so hard for, has dried up like a fresh fruit left in the sun.

Since then, the conflict between Khadija and Mr Asmal has become communal. The panchat aunties wait in anticipation for their next battle. Mr Asmal does not care what everybody thinks. He is happy that his daughter has stayed with him. He holds to her dearly, for she has shaped his present, and she will shape his future. He believes that his role in life is to show people the importance of gratitude. He keeps telling Khadija that her suffering is owing to her anger with Allah – her ungratefulness.

Disappointing news is received not only with tears and anguish – so Mr Asmal tells his wife that he will go to Taj Supermarket. He intends to buy groceries to give as hampers to the men who push trolleys through Lenasia in search of recyclable materials. Khadija scowls and says that he must waste all their hard-earned money on those who need to earn their own livelihoods. If they could earn employment in other ways, why would they resort to dig through garbage in earnest search of recyclable materials, Mr Asmal wonders to himself.

'While you are away, I will go to the maulana's house for the Taalim gathering,' says Khadija as she adjusts her black abaya and drapes the scarf over her greying hair. But Mr Asmal cannot hear her, for he has already left their house.

Khadija fills her days by visiting the sick, bathing new-born babies, and attending religious and social gatherings in the community. Today, she goes to the maulana's house with a different purpose. Khadija struggles on her flat, open-toe black sandals through the grass and red sand that carpets Rose Park to the maulana's house. She gathers up her long black abaya in two-handed fistfuls. A black scarf draped on her head, she turns the beads of a tasbeeh between her index finger and thumb, as older Muslim folk normally do.

Muttering between gasps of air, she rains curses on the ANC government for not maintaining the park. On her right stands the play equipment, its swings hanging unhinged with chains fallen to the ground. She stares beyond the broken equipment to the houses packed together tighter than their coats of coloured paint. Most are single-storeyed, and over the years they have all grown burglar bars on windows, and higher walls with padlocked gates. This is for safety reasons: to keep bad elements out and to keep the inhabitants safely imprisoned. Khadija has begged Mr Asmal to secure their home in the same fashion, but he does not believe in converting their home into a prison. He tells her that he has put his full trust in Allah, the creator and destroyer of all.

She stops and bends down to remove her sandal and empty the stones which have gathered at the toes. A hadada ibis shrieks mercilessly, and she cocks her head in the direction of the sound. The shrill has sent shivers down her spine. For a minute, she is disorientated and contemplates returning home. Sharp light catches her gaze where a young boy lights a cigarette.

Undeniably, Lenasia is a township masked in decay. Life has ceased growing since the country was plunged into darkness by the pandemic beginning in early 2020. The youth have left in the wake of informal settlers scourging the desolate land that lies unused.

Khadija was born in Lenasia. She grew up in Lenasia. Except for the time when she was removed from the jinn who encroached on her soul, she has lived in Lenasia all her life. And she has always despised its ugly appearance.

Maulana Yacoob's home is a badly bruised, purple-coloured council house with a black zinc roof capped by twisting vines which wind down into the frame. In front of the house is a closed veranda with poorly plastered old windows. An ageing, rickety door leads into this space. Wooden benches with red leather seating cling to both walls of the small enclosure. A rumpled, tawny sheet hangs like a curtain, enclosing the entrance to the maulana's small office space. Many a tale meant for the maulana's ears only is delightfully received by those who sit on the red leather benches, anticipating their turn to confide in the spiritual healer.

Behind the maulana's office is his home, extended to now house his nine children and two daughters-in-law. Alongside the house, in a yard enclosed with a tired prefabricated fence, various models of Toyota cars with sale slogans are parked.

Khadija crosses wild weeds which wrap the pavement to reach to the veranda's doorway. Slowly, she climbs the two unevenly cemented steps, enters the enclosure, and joins others who also wait to see the maulana. She slumps down onto the bench and then steadies herself as the wooden legs tremble beneath her weight. The sudden shudder of the bench sends its two young occupants off into the skirts of their mother, who reaches into her bag and pulls out two cellular phones which she gives to the children. Khadija glances at the phones. The screens become animated within touching distance. The children bend their heads over the screens lying in their laps. It is hardly surprising that children these days have become so wayward. It's because they require the instant gratification they receive from technology in their daily play. Khadija scorns this with an air of one exposed to abomination.

When the curtain is pulled sideways and the maulana appears, Khadija stands up to follow him. She casts a disinterested look at the man whose turn it is. The woman with the children rises. She insists that they have been waiting a long time, but Khadija ignores their protests and pushes past a staring maulana, who obediently follows her.

'What is it now, Naani?' he demands.

The maulana is stout with a large protruding belly which

stands out like a hump under his flowing white kurta. He always wears a red-and-white Palestinian scarf draped over his head in a turban. His eyes are adorned with a layer of kohl to ward off all nazr. His large, bushy beard is streaked with silvery grey. Talk has it that in his youth the maulana was disobedient, and much to his mother's sadness, he was sent to India for reformation. He returned home with the esteemed title of being a religious leader bestowed with a gift of exorcism. The maulana had also mastered the art of applying kohl in even layers and making ablution in an eastern toilet without splashing a drop of urine.

Often, he laughs at his daughters when they watch Instagram tutorials to learn the different ways to outline their eyes with eyeliner pencils. He says that the kohl which looks like black shoe polish, hidden within a small green tin, is the best brand, and only the tip of the pinkie finger is needed to make the perfect application. He says that every other eye make-up gadget is a marketing gimmick from the 'West' to injure the eyes. And he should know. He is, after all, a spiritual healer. He is the great Maulana Sahebjee. He beckons them into his presence, then dips the base of his pinkie finger into a tiny green tin of kohl, and rubs it with precision onto the outlines of their eyes.

'Maulana, please don't call me Naani. Rather call me Aunty Khadija,' Khadija protests. Although she is old, and the maulana addresses her with respect, she hates being called 'grandmother' because she believes she will only earn that title once her dear daughter becomes wed and nurses children at her ripe bosom. Why won't Allah give her a son-in-law, and why won't he give her grandchildren like all her friends, who are blessed with titles like Naani and Daadi? Is it fair that now, even though the gullies of old age have crept into her being, she should still own a daughter who remains a spinster?

'No problem, Aunty Khadija, I will still respect you like my own grandmother,' he says. 'Now tell me your problem.'

'Nothing is working!' she cries. 'My daughter remains a spinster. I rubbed the juice of a ripe yellow lemon into her hair and burnt incense as you advised, and nothing has happened. Fa'eeza Asmal has also read Surah Maryam daily for the past forty-one days. What else can be done? Tell me, oh revered

Maulana! Please do tell me!' Fresh tears snake down her cheeks.

The maulana shakes his head and takes out a clean white page from under the counter. He reaches for a pen, jots something down, and passes the paper to Khadija.

'You see,' he says, 'we have ruled out Jaadoo and Nazr. Fa'eeza Asmal is not tainted by jealousy or black magic. Recite this tasbeeh daily. Insha'Allah, only good will come from it.'

Khadija reaches for her spectacles which hang off a chain. She opens them and puts them on. She screws her eyes at the scribbles on the page.

'Is there nothing you can do?' she cries.

The maulana does not take kindly to Khadija's outburst. He lifts his hand to silence her.

Fortunately, Khadija knows not to say anything else. She resumes her old sulk and becomes sombre.

'Ever since Fa'eeza Asmal turned sixteen, things were never right,' she laments. 'This is our fifteenth year in waiting. Mr Asmal dreams of handing over the furniture business to our son-in-law. Only then will he retire. I long to see my baby married. I long to hold my grandchildren... Why won't the suitors propose? Life is so unfair!'

'Maybe it seems not fair now, Aunty Khadija,' says Maulana. 'It's a small test from Allah. Make sabr and be thankful for everything else that Allah has bestowed upon you.'

Khadija scowls. She hates being told to be thankful. Can nobody see the problem they face?

***

It is just as the Zuhr Azaan echoes from the mimbars that Khadija arrives home. Mr Asmal is busy brewing masala tea on the gas stove. He has bought burfee cake from the bakery.

'I didn't know that we had reason to celebrate,' says Khadija as she unwinds the scarf off her head.

Before Mr Asmal can admonish her for her sarcasm, Fa'eeza Asmal walks in. She looks like the 'old maid' she is – which is how the panchat aunties describe her – in a faded, stretched-out black jersey and black tights. She looks like her Foois, her mother tells everybody. She is built large around her buttocks, with tiny breasts – which is good if you are married on the farm with many children but runs counter to your desperate search for Mr Right. She has a longish face and has her waist-length hair pulled back flat into a bun.

Fa'eeza has just come to take her share of tea and cake and regards it as a business meeting with Mr Asmal. Her mother was not happy when she decided to join Mr Asmal in the business. At first, she insisted that no unmarried daughter of hers would cut wood and create furniture. It was unheard of. She argued that Fa'eeza Asmal's place remained within their home, where she would master the finer details of becoming a good wife. She grudgingly gave in when Fa'eeza told her that the furniture buyers would see her, and through word of mouth more Mr Eligibles were likely to request a samoosa run. Fa'eeza Asmal is irritated with her mother's obsession with her getting a proposal. She has long since realised that men do not find her desirable, but she allows suitors to visit because she does not wish to hurt her mother's feelings.

Mr Asmal congratulates Fa'eeza on excellent news.

'You are a great businesswoman,' says her father. 'You are better than any son or son-in-law! Do you know that we got the tender! Alhamdullilah!'

Such talk makes Fa'eeza Asmal proud, and she beams fiercely. She announces that she would like to spend more time in the business.

'That is good thinking, my girl,' says Mr Asmal.

'What! A businesswoman?' cries Khadija. 'You want to run the business! Control it? Fa'eeza Asmal, do you even realise what you are saying?'

'Yes, I do, *Mother!*' responds Fa'eeza icily. 'We got the government tender to furnish the newly built classrooms and homes in the upcoming developments. Do you know what that means? And it was my idea to apply for it! It's wonderful, and Dad needs me more now than ever!'

'Ya Allah! I should never have allowed you to go to the factory! Ya Allah! What have I done? Look at you! Look how you dress! You have become a man! Surely Qiyamat is near! These are the signs – women becoming men! Who will marry you now?' shrieks Khadija, beating her fists into her chest.

'Don't blame yourself, Khadija. It was the right decision to make. We have empowered our daughter. And when my son-in-law comes, he can join us in the business.'

'*Empowered* our daughter? No man wants an *empowered* wife. No man will marry her now,' says Khadija tiredly.

'Ag, Ma, let the whole marriage thing go already, please. Just be happy that we got the tender, Alhamdullilah!' says Fa'eeza Asmal with finality.

It is a burdened night, and Khadija cannot rest. Her eyelids weigh down, but slumber refuses to beckon her. Oh, why is Allah testing her so? Has she not endured enough? When will her punishment end? She despises Mr Asmal, who has purposely added more fuel to the fires which rage within her and yet, he dares to sleep so peacefully.

***

The suitor's name is Bilal – a great-grandson of the esteemed Bulbulia clan which reigns from the densely packed lanes of Fietas. He is the one who was last to nurture in the womb and to suckle from meagre remains left after the thirteen before him devoured their fill. The suitor has lived a reckless life, scavenging in the shadows of his older siblings and doing everything wrong to gain his parents' attention. He was not circumcised at birth, as is custom among Muslims, and when finally at the haphazard age of fourteen the sharpened blade sliced away his foreskin, he wailed like a virgin maiden whose flower has been stolen. On that day, Bilal became a 'Beelooo' announced in jest with a rhythmic twist of the tongue and head. Beeloo loves beautiful, fair-skinned maidens and was the first of all his thirteen siblings to propose to the first woman he set eyes on. She, of course, declined because he did not own a true penny to his name. And then he proposed again to another maiden. And again. But his empty pockets surpass his good looks. For the modern woman, there is no 'lurve' – he is told – for she seeks only a man of financial stability and profession.

Then the news of Mr Asmal's tender grant reaches the ears of the Bulbulia clan, and that of Lenasia, which is home to both families. It reaches the ears of every Muslim family in South Africa.

Beeloo, the girl-ish man. He is now forty-three, yet he still chases maidens and sponges off his older siblings. He broods, knowing that he will only inherit a meagre thirteenth of his father's wealth. As a result, he finds solace in the bosom of his aged mother in a conniving attempt to take the gold which adorns her arms and neck. He decides to remain with her after his brothers and their wives have left. She feeds him and entertains his strange habits. So, he keeps himself happy.

'The thirteenth son of the Bulbulias is up to no good,' the panchat aunties chide. 'His siblings are angered by his outlandish ways. They fear for the family name, but he does not change.'

The news of Mr Asmal, the tender, and the spinster Fa'eeza Asmal finally reaches the overgrown Beeloo. He hears about Fa'eeza Asmal from the chivalrous Ahmad Cassim – Lenasia's very first muezzin. Nicknamed 'Thunderous Voice' in good humour, he is said to have summoned sleeping babies tucked deep into the womb for the Fajr salaah – although one word from him and you knew that the loudspeaker for the call to prayer was probably set on its highest frequency.

'Beeloo, I have heard,' Ahmad whispers in his conversation with Beeloo and the aged Mrs Bulbulia, 'that the son-in-law inherits the Asmal empire.'

One line.

That is all it takes for Bilal 'Beeloo' Bulbulia to offer a proposal to Mr Asmal for Fa'eeza's hand in marriage. Khadija is overjoyed, for she has heard a great deal about the Bulbulias and their beautiful baking and la-di-da ways. What luck. Allah has surely blessed them. Fa'eeza has no say in the matter, for she had been pledged to the first man to offer her his hand in matrimony. So Beeloo it will have to be.

There is no doubt in Beeloo's mind why he wants to marry Fa'eeza Asmal. His thirteen siblings have tried to talk him out of it. 'Her father is not foolish; he will not give you a cent of his wealth. He will make you slog for his business and pay you nothing. The girl is a plain ageing simpleton. What are you thinking, young brother?'

But Beeloo is unwavering in his determination to marry Fa'eeza Asmal. He is sworn to secrecy by Khadija, who has promised him the Asmal dynasty if he were to wed her daughter. He can't remember her exact words, but she mentioned him breaking a curse of sorts. He wonders what she means and regrets now that he did not ask her, but he abolishes the thought. He does not worry. He knows the power of a man over his wife.

After Khadija's enthusiastic response to the proposal is conveyed back to Beeloo, after the correct garb is purchased for Fa'eeza Asmal to wear, a date is set for the nikaah. In the minutes leading up to this union, Beeloo feels his heartbeat quicken almost rapidly, like the second hand on a clock. He wonders about the beckoning years.

***

Beeloo sees Fa'eeza Asmal for the first time in their bridal bedchamber. She sits on the bed, the folds of material from her golden bridal garara arranged around her. Her hair falls in vast waves over her shoulders. She keeps her head bowed, completely oblivious of his presence. All the while she is reciting softly, 'Ya-salaamoo, Ya-salaamoo, Ya-salaamoo – peace, peace, peace.' She then puts her henna-painted hands together and appears to examine the dainty artwork. 'Oh Allah!' she pleads, 'please give me strength to endure a loveless marriage.'

Beeloo is struck with curiosity.

She is a phantom personified, a heavenly woman of alluring sadness reaching out to him, drawing him closer.

Beeloo tries to avert his gaze, but he cannot. He is trapped. Her beauty denies the occasion. They cannot mourn. Her coy, endearing innocence shouts out to him, and without thinking, he reaches to hug her. She staggers back, and he collapses – his head caving into the folds of material which cloak her bare thighs. He looks up and stares into the frightened eyes of a timid deer. His eyes dissolve into a smile, and Fa'eeza Asmal hastily straightens her back. Beeloo is captivated by this woman. He speaks to her in gentle tones about everything and yet nothing. She does not let on that she feels uncomfortable in his presence and remains fully clothed, the heavy jewellery weighing down onto her awkward frame.

Beeloo leaves the room and joins his mother, who is drinking masala tea with naan-katai. She recounts the wedding reception. From what she says, it sounds like a grand affair. He listens attentively to his mother when she recalls Fa'eeza Asmal's heart-wrenching sobs when she bade her father farewell.

The image of a bridal Fa'eeza Asmal again captures his thoughts. He becomes breathless when he thinks of her. He does not lust after her. He is drawn to the alluring essence within her. Perhaps she is the nurturing soul he needs to help him heal from his old ways? Sudden fear grips him because he is expected to remain detached from her. After all, she is merely a business deal – nothing more.

A single chip of toasted almond in the naan-katai catches that thought. Beeloo chokes. He coughs uncontrollably. He struggles to breathe. He sees his mother's frightened eyes. She pushes a glass of water to him, and he knocks it over. Water falls. The glass breaks into pieces at his feet. He tears at his throat with his fingers. He doubles over, and she thumps his back. Beeloo rakes at the phantom claws which threaten to strangle him. And in those final seconds, he pleads to Allah and makes many a promise. He promises to earn Fa'eeza Asmal's trust and to love only her until death parts them.

Beeloo observes a miracle then. As sudden as the clouds dissipate after a thunderstorm, he feels well again. He spits the roasted almond chip into his palm, admiring its strength. He is in awe of Allah's greatness. Allah had used this insignificant object to cripple him into total submission.

Happiness swells in his chest.

He returns to his betrothed then. She is asleep. Her form, still fully clothed. Her hair lies draped across the pillow. He covers her with a soft blanket. Beeloo then retires to the bathroom where he bathes. He dons the bridal pyjamas purchased for him by his sisters. When he emerges from the bathroom, the curtains have extended inwards, shivering with the icy wind. He hears the drumming beat from the branches of trees knocking at the window panes. He hears laughter, high pitched and haunting. Beeloo watches Fa'eeza Asmal spin around, her head thrown back, her arms reaching backwards, her hair festooned around her. He reaches for her then and embraces her. He prays, Surah Naas loudly.

She beats her fists into his chest. Her finger nails claw at his face. Her eyes remain closed but her eyeballs wage war within. He completes the prayer and blows over her. She grows limp as the fight leaves her. The wind dies down and the trees lower their branches.

She opens her eyes.

Birds Kept in Cages, Curse...

Juleikha's eyes flutter open, and a shiver cascades down the full length of her body into the soles of her ageing feet. She anticipates the events of the day soon to unfold. It is the most auspicious day of the week, *Jummah* Friday – when, once a week, she performs ablution of the full body and washes the coconut oil off her hair before her early morning prayers. The moonlight cascades through the naked windows, casting silhouettes onto the whitewashed walls of her room. The neon green hands of her small, rectangular-faced alarm clock point to the twelve and three. She needs time on her side today, as she has far too much to do. Juleikha climbs out of bed, places her feet into her sandals, and heads in the dark to the bathroom. On her way, she reaches for the steel hanger on the cupboard door handle that holds her Friday attire. She closes the door behind her and places the hanger carefully on the steel screw knocked in at an awkward angle into the height of the door. She takes out a pink plastic comb from the front breast pocket of her dress and places it on the frame of the bath, near the tap.

Still dressed in her full-length white nightdress with embroidered lace at the edges, Juleikha carefully climbs into the bath and sits on the wooden stool facing the tap. She allows only a trickle of water to pass through, then gasps – the water is icy cold. With both hands, she reaches for the heavy bar of green Sunlight soap and rubs it into a lather of white foam. This she smears on a pumice rock and then with her right hand, reaches under the thin wet cotton nightdress close to her bosom, for her left underarm. She scrubs the skin in the pit of her arm almost viciously to wash out all the dirt that has settled there. When she is satisfied that both her underarms are clean, she rubs off the dry skin under her feet.

Beyond the bathroom window, the early morning birds begin to chirp, reminding Juleikha that time for prayer is fast approaching. As if beckoned to their call, she hurriedly unties her long, silver-black plait and combs out the knots that have nested there. She reaches for the pink plastic jug that sits on the rim of the bath, protected in the corner, by the mosaic tiles on the wall, and half fills it with warm water.

Then she bends her head down and tips the jug over her head, allowing the water to flow over and drip down into the drain. Again, she reaches for the green bar of soap which she rubs directly into her scalp, massaging the soap into her hair. Juleikha then opens the tap and sticks her head under. Using all her fingers, she scrubs her hair clean, pulls the strands together, and squeezes the water free. Next, she fastens her green hand towel with the frayed edging tightly around her hair. Juleikha stands up slowly and, placing her right leg out first, she climbs out of the bath. She uses both hands to hold onto the steel shower pole in front of her.

Her now-wet nightdress clinging to her form, she quickly removes her water-soaked panty from under the nightdress and puts on a clean, dry cotton one. Juleikha then unbuttons the nightdress and lets it fall to the floor. She keeps on her wet bra; it will dry soon in the hot December sun. Juleikha slips a clean and long satin, emerald-green dress with matching trousers – her Friday best – over her head. She squeezes the towel around her hair to remove the excess water, then she removes the towel from her hair and bends down to wipe the water that has collected on the floor. Her wet night-clothes and her towel she throws into a plastic bucket which she stores under the black plumbing of the basin sink. She will wash them, later, when the sun paints the sky yellow and bright blue. Juleikha collects her pink comb and returns to the silent confines of her room.

Juleikha is the only one awake in the house – her daughter, son, and daughter-in-law sleep on. It is best to keep everything peaceful and quiet until the house wakes to the bustle of the day. The call for prayer echoes into the night sky. Juleikha rolls out her prayer mat to face the Kiblah, the sacred mosque in Makah.

From her cupboard, she carefully pulls out her white hijab with the neat pink flowers patterned on the border. Her hair is still wet and lies in clumps at her nape. She wears the hijab over her head and tightens the elastic at the neck. Patiently, she waits for the final words of the call for prayer before she performs the early morning prayers. She raises both hands together and prays that the pot of biryani that she will later prepare for her daughter Safiyyah's year-end function will be delicious and well received.

Juleikha then removes her hijab and her emerald-green dress and replaces it with a satin slip, and over it her beige-coloured checked apron with the short sleeves. With her comb, she brushes her silver-black hair, threading it neatly into a plait which rests on her straight, proud back. From her cupboard she takes out a square scarf, folds it into a triangle, places it over her head, and ties it below her chin. At fifty, Juleikha looks old; her harsh life has eaten her youth and left her with deep wrinkles, sagging skin, and a bitterness which she wears as gracefully as she can.

The first to awaken is the parrot, Zeyn, and in his cage he shrieks, 'Norr...ma...wethu! Nomawethu!' Nomawethu is Juleikha's neighbour and only friend. Zeyn's large cage is placed on a small wooden table, in the corner of the dining room, alongside the deep freezer. Juleikha removes the black sheet which covers his cage. After she opens the cage door, she reaches for the bowl which holds seeds. Zeyn's grey feathers spread out, and he jerks forward. Juleikha backs away from the cage – shocked. Zeyn appears to be attacking her. His unusual behaviour worries Juleikha. She hopes he is not ill.

Once in the kitchen, she fills his seed bowl, and from the kitchen window, Juleikha sees that her neighbour's house lights are switched on. An inner peace settles with the knowledge that Zeyn has completed his morning duty of waking the neighbours for the day ahead. Nomawethu does not believe that the bird possesses any sense. She argues that that's what parrots do. She prophesises bad omens when birds are kept caged and often insists that Juleikha let the bird free.

When she returns to the dining room, Zeyn sits upright on

the edge of the wooden perch of his swing, which moves back and forth slowly. Jolted back to the present, Juleikha watches Zeyn's eyes target the bowl which she holds firmly in her hands.

Zeyn is restless and squawks again. 'Nomawethu! Nomawethu!' He spreads his wings and then soars towards the cage bars. Juleikha lets out a frightened scream. She instinctively holds out her hands in front of her, rocking on the balls of her feet to steady herself. She opens the cage door and throws in the bowl, scattering seeds everywhere. Zeyn stops his anxious fluttering and falls forward, into the dropped seeds. His body stops heaving, and he becomes very still. Juleikha is frozen to the spot.

The noise has woken Safiyyah, Hoosein, and Rahma. Juleikha watches them coming down the passage.

'What happened?' chorus Hoosein and Safiyyah.

Rahma stands in her husband's embrace.

'I have no idea,' mumbles Juleikha. She reaches for Safiyyah's hand. 'Zeyn... seems possessed...'

'Ag, Ma. You know that you are not making sense, right.' Hoosein opens the door of the cage and prods at the bird's body with his fingers. 'He's breathing. I will take him to the vet on my way to work. Moenie worry nie, all right? Alles sal eventually regkom.'

Juleikha agrees that it is best that Hoosein takes Zeyn to the doctor. Hoosein reaches for Rahma's hand and leads her back to their bedroom. Safiyyah pulls out a chair from beneath the dining room table and gently nudges Juleikha into it. She then disappears into the kitchen.

'Safiyyah,' Juleikha calls out. 'Let's use the Royal Albert tea set today. I feel like I need a good omen before setting your biryani.'

'Mummy, Zeyn will be well soon. Mark my words,' Safiyyah says in earnest. 'He's probably just allergic to something. Bhai will sort everything out.'

'I hope that it's just that, Safiyyah! Please make a special prayer, okay, and tell the children you teach to also send prayers for my darling Zeyn.'

Juleikha wipes her wet eyes with the loose material of her

head scarf. 'You know, my child, I don't want to say anything bad, and Allah must forgive me if I am wrong, but I think that this has happened to my poor Zeyn because of Aunty Nomawethu's bad thoughts...' Juleikha frowns. 'She never liked my Zeyn! She always warns that locking a bird in a cage alone is cruel, and birds bestow ill wishes on their owner, but I think she just doesn't like him.'

'No, no, no, Ma. Come on now. It's nothing like that. Zeyn will be well soon, you will see. I need to go get ready now, okay. You will be okay? We will collect the food at eleven-thirty, okay?'

Safiyyah collects the teacups and places them on the tray.

'Eleven...' Juleikha repeats, deep in thought. She contemplates not making the biryani. Surely, she should rather sit on the musallah in prayer for Zeyn's recovery. It is, after all, a *Jummah* morning. She then re-considers as she has promised Safiyyah that she would cook the meal, and she can't break her promise now.

Safiyyah bends down to hug her, but she pulls away.

'Just pray that my Zeyn is okay.'

Safiyyah does not respond. Juleikha watches her leave the room, balancing the tray with the dainty cups on her outstretched arms. Juleikha gets up and heads over to the cage. She strains her ears against the bars to listen to the sound of the bird's heartbeat. Everything is quiet. Without fully realising it, she begins to pray. She opens the door to the cage, blows into her open palms and gently rubs her hands over his full form. Zeyn's body stirs a few minutes later.

'You see, Ma, he's okay.' Hoosein stands behind Juleikha. 'I phoned Dr Lategaan, and he said to bring Zeyn in at 9am. Alles sal eventually regkom, Ma. Remember that, okay.'

'I guess you are right, my child. Let me go prepare Safiyyah's biryani. It's getting late.'

Juleikha goes to the kitchen, grateful for the biryani-making task which will occupy her mind for the morning.

In the kitchen, Juleikha switches on the radio to the voice of Bongwani Bingwa on the 702 morning show. She picks up the kitchen stool with two hands and carries it to the grocery cupboard. The olive-green leather has lifted at the edges, and the leather cuts into her palms. The naked leg tips of the worn stool meet the white porcelain tiles with a soft clang. When Rahma moved in, she made Hoosein remove the linoleum flooring from the house and replace it with porcelain tiles. She had lamented that linoleum flooring was extremely old-fashioned. Juleikha had no say in the matter. Rahma was aware that Hoosein had received the house as inheritance when his father had passed away. On the day the porcelain tiles were placed, Juleikha had received a pair of pink rubber-soled sandals from Nomawethu.

Juleikha holds onto the cupboard door handle and pulls herself up into standing position onto the stool's green head. She rises tall to the cupboard's height, then with two hands, reaches for the large steel pot which she stores at the top of the grocery cupboard. She cradles the pot with one hand to her bosom before climbing down.

Safiyyah enters and waits until Juleikha has placed the pot on the tabletop before she speaks. 'Ma, you don't listen.' She points at the stool. 'I told you to call me to get the pot for you. You could fall and injure yourself.'

Juleikha smiles. 'I know, my child. I don't want to trouble you. I know that you are busy. And I managed, see.'

'Ma, I know, but next time, ask Hoosein or Rahma or somebody please, okay.'

Juleikha rolls her eyes. 'Rahma? Rahma will throw my stools away before she gets a chance to stand on them, let alone get the pot down for me!'

'Ma... Okay, just ask Bhai then, but please don't do it again yourself.'

'Okay, Dadimaa,' Juleikha teases. 'Now hurry. You going to be late for the last day of school, and teachers can't arrive late.'

Safiyyah laughs. 'Thanks, Ma. Salaam. I will see you at eleven-ish to collect the food, okay.'

In the past, Juleikha had always kept hens in her yard, and when it was needed, she would go out into the chicken-run, grab the squawking hens by their necks, and haul them into the house where she would, with mastered skill, sever the jugular vein without cutting the oesophagus or windpipe. It was only later, when Safiyyah began working, that Juleikha started buying cut, unwashed chickens from the butchery. She washed them herself because she lamented that the 'washed chickens' still held too many bloody veins. Juleikha had marinated five chickens cut into large biryani-sized pieces early on Thursday morning because the meat had to marinate well in the spices. She had also boiled the lentils and stored them in the fridge, in their colander.

Now she pours fifteen cups of water into a large deep pot and places the pot on high heat, covering two plates on the gas stove. She heaves the ten-kilogram rice tin from the lowest shelf in the cupboard and slides it onto the floor at her feet. As a child, Juleikha would always imagine herself dancing with the sari-clad ladies painted in blue on the tin. When her mother passed away, Juleikha had requested that the tin be gifted to her. She had worried that her sister-in-law would throw it away.

She teases off the lid and watches as it falls from her fingers to the floor. With a teacup, she fills and pours one cup after the other, totalling ten cups of rice, into a plastic bowl. Juleikha carries the bowl to the basin and places it under the open tap to allow the water to cover the grains. With her fingers, she plays with the grains of rice, rubbing off the dirt. She empties the milky white water, fills water into the bowl again, and then repeats the process two more times. Then she empties the rice from the bowl into the pot of boiling water. Using a large dessert spoon, she stirs the rice into the water. She tilts the lid onto the pot, allowing some space for the steam to escape, then continues to guard the pot, attentively observing the bubbling, hot water as it allows the rice to surface like shimmering shells on the shore. When the rice is almost cooked, Juleikha empties the rice from the pot into a large colander she has placed into a basin bowl. The rice is left there to drain.

Juleikha collects coiled rolls of outdated newspapers from the sack which hangs behind the kitchen door. These sheets she spreads out on the zinc basin top. She takes ten medium-sized potatoes from the vegetable rack and busies herself with the tedious task of peeling and cutting the potatoes into quarters using the sharp knife Nomawethu had gifted her. At the time, Juleikha had felt sceptical about accepting the knife. Receiving a knife as a gift only meant bad news. Now, many moons later, as the sharp-bladed knife glides over the potato skin in swift movements, Juleikha is deeply appreciative to her friend for the gift.

Almost immediately, Juleikha's thoughts shift to Nomawethu and then to... Zeyn. Her eyes dart around – searching. With the back of her hand, she wipes the beads of sweat from her forehead. *Does keeping a bird mean bad news? Or is it Nomawethu's bad thoughts that have made Zeyn ill? What if something bad is going to happen?*

These thoughts agitate her. She presses her palms onto the newspaper-clothed basin top and her forehead against the warm skin of the window. Nomawethu's kitchen lies beyond the palisade wall that separates the houses. Although far from them, Juleikha can still see the tiny, tensed faces in the kitchen, the impatient bodies in school uniforms with not enough space to manoeuvre their way out the backdoor to school. In the doorway, Nomawethu stands with a tower of lunch packs in her outstretched hands. She looks tired, much older than her years. When Juleikha sees her, her heart dissolves into a sudden yearning. She feels a strange longing for emotional comfort. She opens her mouth, bewildered.

'Nomawethu!' she screams, banging on the window with the open palm of her hand.

Nomawethu does not hear her. Or look up. She puts the lunch bags onto the counter next to her, watching as they collapse in scattered parcels onto the floor at her feet. Her large form hunches forward in a desperate attempt to try to salvage the food from hurried feet.

Juleikha's face twists, she strains her eyes, and creases her forehead, allowing deep lines to furrow across it. Never has she felt so alone, so afraid of what was to become of her Zeyn... and of her.

'Nomawethu!' she whimpers. Her voice is nothing but a throaty whine, caught in limbo between the thick windows of both homes.

Nomawethu stands up, holding tattered bread slices and slimy tomato, the remnants of the sandwiches she has made for her many children. She begins to walk away from the back door, into the cave of her kitchen. Juleikha watches, wide-eyed, as her silhouette dwindles into the hazy morning sunlight before she melts away.

Juleikha's palm stays stuck to the window, against the background of an open door and a trail of anxious-faced children tripping over loose shoelaces, racing to school.

Juleikha averts her gaze to see Rahma's stony form standing in the doorway of the kitchen. Hoosein is not with her. She steals a glance at Juleikha, only to immediately look away. Her manner hurts Juleikha. There is always resentment in her black-smeared eyes. Rahma places Zeyn's seed bowl on the kitchen table.

'Rahma, my child. Where is Hoosein?'

'He is collecting the bird's cage. We are leaving now.'

Juleikha says, 'What about breakfast? It will take me only two minutes...'

Rahma's foot hits the table leg, and it screeches angrily to match her mood. She stands directly in front of Juleikha, her eyes fixed on her. 'We will be late. We still have to take the bird to the vet. And, anyway, the smell of this kitchen makes me feel rather ill.'

Juleikha has not expected Rahma's harsh tone. It dawns on her that Rahma not having breakfast has nothing to do with Zeyn or being late for work. It has nothing to do with the smell of cooking food. It is simply due to Rahma's pity for her; she sees the fear that snakes through Juleikha's soul.

'I see,' Juleikha says finally.

It looks like Rahma wants to say more. Her hazel eyes are laden with words, with rebukes. But she doesn't say anything.

Juleikha kisses Rahma on the forehead and quietly returns to the kitchen basin as Hoosein appears at the kitchen entrance, holding a cage covered in a black cloth.

'Oh good, Ma, you look okay now,' Hoosein says. 'Rahma has made you smile, I see. That is good.'

'Hoosein, my son, Rahma was just telling me, she—'

Hoosein waits for her to complete her sentence, but it seems as if something has changed in the colour of his eyes. A thought, fear, the unspeakable, clambers around them. His handsome, clean-shaven face falls. There is no longer purpose to bring joy to the moment.

'We are going,' he says abruptly. 'I will let you know what Dr Lategaan says. Salaam, Ma.'

'Go well, my son,' Juleikha mumbles.

Barely able to stand, Juleikha lowers her shaky body onto the green-headed stool. The fluorescent light on the ceiling flickers between bright and hazy. Her eyes burn with tears. She must present a pitiful sight. An unwanted presence.

An uninvited image rises in her mind. Of herself, dressed in a red sari, gold bangles chiming on her stretched-out arms, running through the cotton fields in India. It all feels so long ago. Who was she then? What had happened to that Juleikha, with her determined thoughts and her joyful spirit?

Drawn back to the moment, Juleikha lets out a sigh. She feels light-headed and leans back against the basin. The view of the table wanders into her vision. The biryani! She stands up. Her movements are measured, as if she is afraid of breaking away like rocks being weathered – bit by bit, filtering into the wind. She closes and opens her fists, licks her lips. Her throat is dry and scratchy. The sounds of running feet and children talking have died down. By now, Nomawethu's children have probably left for school. Juleikha's attention returns to the potatoes which lie naked to the sun, turning grey. She takes out a deep pot from under the kitchen basin and places it on the stove. She bends down again to remove a cream-coloured enamel oil container. Once she has poured oil into the pot, she turns the knob on the gas plate and watches as the circumference of the plate erupts into a blue flame. It has always amazed Juleikha to see the plate flare up on the gas hob. She grew up using a coal stove, and she often feels astounded by the changes in technology.

Rahma once told her to 'get with the times' – Hoosein had assured her that Rahma meant well, but Juleikha did not like her daughter-in-law's condescending tone. She feels assured knowing that Safiyyah will honour the family and home into which she marries.

Juleikha throws a teaspoon of turmeric into the cut potato

wedges which wait in the bowl. With her bare hand, she tosses the potatoes until they are all tinted yellow. Carefully, she lifts handfuls of yellow-tinted potatoes and places them into the pot of hot oil. Using a large colander serving spoon, Juleikha stirs the potatoes into the bubbling liquid. While she watches, the potato wedges transform into glistening gold. Then she spreads two sheets of paper towel onto a plate and scoops out the fried potato wedges onto the paper towel to drain.

It is early December, and the morning sun's rays have already burnt the horizon. Juleikha pulls at the fabric of her sleeves close to her underarms, allowing air to stream through, gently cooling her skin. She opens the fridge door and lets the cool air wash over her, then takes the ghee canister from the fridge and places it next to the large pot on the kitchen table's green melamine surface. Juleikha pulls the large enamel dish which holds the marinating pieces of chicken out of the fridge. The net cloth covering the chickens is now drenched in glistening beads of oils and marinade. Last, she takes out the colander of lentils and places it on the table. Juleikha is now ready to set the biryani.

She softly murmurs a prayer. From the ghee canister she spoons out six heaped dessertspoons full of the molten golden ghee into the pot. She then packs the marinated pieces of dripping chicken into the melted ghee. She adds spoons full of the marinade to coat the chicken pieces. The black lentils are tossed into the leftover marinade which lies in the bed of the plastic bowl, which she then scatters randomly onto the marinated chicken pieces. She does the same with the potato wedges. Then she takes half of the rice and throws it into the marinade, mixing all the grains of rice into spices. The kitchen breathes around her, through her, and in her. The deep aroma of the spicy marinade intoxicates her, and she sighs. Juleikha spreads the marinated rice over the chicken and then throws the plain rice over, covering the many spots of colour. She spoons more ghee onto the rice, empties three cups of water into the pot, and secures a sheet of foil over it to mask its contents. She switches on the stove to high and rotates the pot on the flame, waiting for steam to rise above the rice. She then lowers the heat to the lowest. The biryani will cook on low heat.

The mid-morning sunlight sprays through the kitchen windows. Juleikha drifts to its beckoning, peering through the closed glass. She wants to know where Nomawethu is. Over the white-washed, prefabricated fence, the umbrella-shaped steel washing line sways on its pole – naked to the wind. A flight of birds soars through the bright blue sky to perch on the steel, spiderweb-shaped lines, squawking as they do so.

Although Juleikha was not born here, Lenasia has always been her home, where she feels she belongs. Juleikha loves the township with its narrow roads and busy streets. The houses huddle close together, and their occupants take pride in knowing everybody else's stories. She loves it so much that she refuses to move when Hoosein suggests that they do. *Ma, this is not what we fought for when we sought freedom. We are more jailed now, behind our burglar bars. Crime is taking over our lives. Do we wait to be a statistic?*

She often contemplates his words. *A statistic?*

She tells them to go, assures them that she will be fine, but they stay and torture her with harsh gazes and unspoken grievances. Juleikha lets out a sigh. She is exhausted. She has grown so old so fast. She sits slumped on the stool with her back to the kitchen table. Her eyes are closed. Such dejection overcomes her that she can barely move. She thinks that she has heard the door opening, but she is not sure.

'Sanibona Julie,' Nomawethu sings. 'Ninjani? The biryani smells absolutely divine!' She is a voluptuous woman garbed in a satin nightdress with an apron over. Her curly hair is just like Juleikha's, hidden beneath a doek.

'Sanibona, my friend. I thought I heard the door opening.' Juleikha's voice is weak, hesitant.

Without lifting her body, she fumbles with the fingers in her clasp. 'My Zeyn is sick. Hoosein took him to the vet. There's been no phone call, as yet. What's the time?' She searches frantically for the kitchen clock which hangs on the wall of the doorway. 'It's already twenty past ten! Oh, Allah, I hope that all is well with him.'

'Oh no! What happened to Zeyn, Julie?'

'I don't know. He just fell, fainted, I think. He is not...dead. Because there was a heartbeat.'

'He will be okay! I'm sure that Hoosein will call in a bit with good news. What time is Safiyyah collecting the delicious food?'

'Such a big worry! Safiyyah will come now. Eleven, she said.' Juleikha straightens her back against the basin and nods. 'I need to get this kitchen cleaned before they come.'

'Come, I will help you.'

Glass cups with paintings of delicate blue flowers from the Royal Albert tea set clink against the saucers as Juleikha arranges them in the basin sink to be washed.

'The kids left for school today, and I was just thinking that how will I cope with them at home for the holidays? Is my house a hostel? They finish me! But Niq keeps saying that their parents helped when he was young. Now it's his turn to pay back. This Black Tax is killing me. What must I do? I feel so exhausted all the time!' Nomawethu pauses. She takes a deep breath and tries to swallow the sob that vibrates within her. 'I feel helpless in my life.'

On the breeze drifting in through the open door come fading sounds – the revving of a car's engine, the laughter of children playing, the distant call of a bird.

'We all feel that way sometimes.' Juleikha lifts her eyes, her hands now fixed on top of the silver-edged cups. 'I feel the same way since Hoosein's wedding.'

Juleikha looks away from Nomawethu. She wishes she could be somewhere else, at the beach perhaps, sitting in view of the ocean, content and at peace. She stands there, listening to Nomawethu lament, impaled by depression and exhaustion. She wishes that Nomawethu would leave.

'Let me go clean the bedrooms, it's Friday today. You will never get done,' Nomawethu says. With quickened steps, she moves towards the passage.

'I will clean Hoosein's room,' Juleikha calls after her. 'He wouldn't want somebody else in his room.'

'Moenie worry, I will clean Hoosein's room. I know.' Nomawethu laughs. 'There are probably panties strewn across the floor. That child, Rahma. She must clean her own room.

Sies man.'

'You know...' Juleikha sighs.

'Ja, I have breasts and everything else, okay. Ek weet. I will help you. We will get done quickly.'

Juleikha watches her friend disappear into Hoosein's bedroom. She caresses the saucers with a dishcloth, stacks them, and then very carefully, places them into the cupboard under lock and key before following Nomawethu out to the bedrooms.

'Call Hoosein. You will feel better once you know.'

Juleikha pulls out her cellphone from her apron pocket and calls Hoosein.

'Salaam. Hello, Hoosein, Hoosein can you hear me? How's Zeyn doing?'

'Ma, gee I can. Don't scream into the phone. Zeyn is sick...'

'Did Dr Lategaan say what's wrong with him?'

'No, Ma. But they will keep him there tonight. I got to go now, Ma.'

'Okay, insha'allah! Please make duah bheta.'

Hoosein cuts the call. Juleikha is irritated. He didn't even greet. She sighs.

'What does he say?' Nomawethu asks.

'Noma, the doctor doesn't know what is wrong with Zeyn! They will keep him there and see.'

'Don't worry, jy sal sien. It will be okay...'

The dark mood dwells in the wake of a thunderstorm. Juleikha is unhappy. The gate screeches a warning on the stone driveway.

'What time is it? Eleven-thirty already?' Juleikha gasps. She rushes to the back door and pulls it open. She needs to tell Safiyyah about Zeyn.

'Safiy—' She stops. She feels Nomawethu's presence behind her.

They enter, hand in hand through the steel doorframe. Juleikha's heart hammers hard. Her gaze remains lowered as she stares quite rudely at Safiyyah's fingers entwined with the fingers of a salmon-pink-skinned man.

She feels Nomawethu's elbows in her waist, nudging her.

Juleikha looks up.

He smiles. His curly hair is hidden beneath a black crocheted prayer hat, giving a certain seriousness to his clean-shaven face. He wears a dark-grey suit like he is the best man at a wedding or perhaps a *groom*. A tremor storms through Juleikha as a hundred thoughts bounce around in her mind. She has barely enough time to unclasp her fingers before he grabs her hand and places two kisses on her cheeks.

'Hello, Mum. I am Michael, I am so happy to finally meet you.' She is baffled by him calling her *mother*. She averts her gaze from Michael's laughing eyes to Safiyyah, who looks tense, screwing her eyes the way Juleikha knows so well, something she does when she is nervous. *Is there something that I am missing here? Safiyyah has never mentioned a Michael before.* Juleikha is overtaken by fatigue and exasperation. A deluge of annoyance rises within her; she has had enough. She wishes to be left in peace. She is exhausted.

'I expect that you are here to carry the heavy hot pot of biryani to the car,' Juleikha says. 'The rice is already steamed. Dish from the bottom. The marinade is there.'

She pushes past them and with long, quickened strides, heads to the steel cabinet. From the bottom drawer, she takes out a large bed sheet and folds the sheet along the centre to create a square. She places the square on the basin top, switches off the blue flame, and carries the heavy pot to the basin, where she places it in the centre of the cloth. She pulls the corners together to make a knot at the centre. Now clothed, the pot still feels hot in her clasp. Juleikha grabs two dish cloths from the drawer and places them on top of the wrapped pot.

Nomawethu is chatting to them.

'Safiyyah! You look prettier by the day!' Nomawethu gushes.

'Thank you, Aunty Nomawethu.'

'Yes! She is truly beautiful!' Michael says. 'And...that's why I love her so...'

Juleikha feels bile rise to her mouth. She struggles to breathe. *Love!* 'Safiyyah! No! No! No! He is not Muslim!'

'Julie!' Nomawethu is shocked.

'Mum, please Mum... Let me explain... He loves me!'

'I love your daughter, Mrs Essop! I will become a good Muslim. I promise. Safiyyah will teach me.'

'No! No! I will never allow my only daughter to marry like this!'

'Mum,' Safiyyah pleads. 'You cannot keep me caged like you keep Zeyn.'

She stares at Safiyyah. *How dare she!* She lashes out at her then.

She is surprised that Michael steps between them. She watches how he reaches for her. She catches the small movement of his lips. There is something comforting in his smile, as if he means it to heal opened wounds.

No one says anything. When Nomawethu reaches for Juleikha, she leans away. She averts her gaze. She turns away and flees them.

***

Hours later, Hoosein opens the door and enters Juleikha's room. The room has slowly dissolved into darkness. Silence dwells in the looming shadows around him. He calls Juleikha; there is no answer. He stands in the doorway and absorbs the stillness, so piercing, he fears to venture forth. Something feels terribly wrong.

His eyes adjust to the inimical blackness, and he sees her small form sitting on the prayer mat. She is holding her covered head between her hands.

'Salaam, Ma, what's wrong?' He turns on the light and drops to her side.

Juleikha lifts her puffy eyes and blinks in the sudden blaze of light. He envelopes her body into his hold. She succumbs to him.

Then slowly the words tumble from the depths of her soul. She sobs helplessly, beating her chest with both fists.

Listening to her, Hoosein is overwhelmed by a twist of severed emotions – anger, shame, and pity. He watches her dissolving face, and he feels helpless. He quietens her fists in his firm hold.

For a long while, Juleikha weeps quietly. Her face is pale, with a strange expression. It is the look of a woman who is besieged by something within, something bigger than anything he has ever known.

The hum of the fan which spins on the ceiling weaves into the silence. They hear the barking of dogs running the streets.

'Allah knows best, Ma. Only *He* is the best of all planners,' he says softly.

For a moment, Juleikha says nothing. She continues to look down at her captive fists.

'Nomawethu knew,' she says.

Hoosein looks at her puzzled. He waits.

'She warned me that birds kept in cages, curse...' She sighs, closes her eyes, and turns away from him.

A Womb Barren

Shaazia lay, spread-eagled on the sterile white crisp sheets, and shivered involuntarily. She nibbled at the skin inside her cheek, praying that she could cover herself once more.

'Place the sheet over your legs,' Dr Selvin, draped in a white coat, instructed. 'Lift them and open wide.'

Another shiver cascaded over Shaazia's full body. All she really wanted was to put on her panty and to bring her legs together, but Dr Selvin had placed a speculum into her vagina as he aspirated mucous from her cervical canal and spread it onto a glass slide.

'Once we find out what these sperms have been up to, we can make further decisions,' Dr Selvin went on, as though he was telling her about the weather. 'Now open your legs as wide as possible.'

Although Dr Selvin spoke in a matter-of-fact tone, Shaazia could sense that he was uncomfortable. Shaazia was adorned in the full hijab, with her eyes also hidden behind a black net.

'Wider please,' he demanded, as Shaazia drew a deep breath and shuddered. 'I just need one more sample.'

Sensing his irritation, Shaazia responded, and Dr Selvin removed the speculum and dropped the white sheet over her legs. Even before Dr Selvin could tell Shaazia to dress, she reached for her underwear from the chair where she had put them, which brought creases to Dr Selvin's aged forehead. Quickly, he packed up his slides before leaving the room. Dr Selvin no doubt knew that the middle-aged husband was sitting unconcerned in the waiting room. The commentary of the cricket match from the smartphone Mr Abdul held in his palms was audible.

'I'm sorry, Mr Abdul. The sperm have not managed to survive,' Dr Selvin announced as he settled into his chair. Shaazia looked at her husband. His expression hadn't changed. Shaazia shrank deeper into her covering, as she lowered her form onto the chair beside her husband.

'Go on.' Dr Selvin motioned. 'Have a look into the microscope. The sperm are not moving.'

Mr Abdul gave him a questioning look, but curious, he bent down to gaze into the microscope. Shaazia, sensing her husband's uneasiness, shifted uncomfortably in her chair. Her husband frowned.

'There's nothing happening here.' Hastily, Mr Abdul stood up and beckoned Shaazia to the microscope.

She sensed Dr Selvin watching them and felt disconcerted knowing that he judged the awkwardness that oozed between them like pus from a wound.

'Dr Selvin, what's happening here?' She stiffens, still absorbing the sight before her.

Dr Selvin gave her a small nod. 'The sperm are not moving, dead.' He twisted a pencil in his hands. 'The environment within you has caused that. It's hostile. We will need to do a laparoscopy to find the reasons for this happening and take it from there. I understand that you want to conceive a baby, and at thirty-four you are not getting younger.' He continued to twirl the pencil before him. Then he looked up and met Mr Abdul's hard stare.

'We will solve your problem of infertility.' Dr Selvin's voice was filled with years of pride, of his expertise in this area.

Shaazia lifted her head. Her eyes, hidden behind the veil, shimmered with fresh tears. 'Thank you so much, Doctor!'

'Thank you,' Dr Selvin said. 'Please go to the front desk and book the earliest appointment for the lap. At your age, we really do not have time to play.'

'I am sorry.' Shaazia's voice crackled with melancholy.

'An operation is unnecessary,' said Mr Abdul. 'Surely you can prescribe some drugs to cure her problem.' His voice rose. 'Next you will tell us that we need to do IVF or some other mumbo jumbo.'

'Mr Abdul, we may need to resort to IVF. We don't know at this point,' Dr Selvin replied. Shaazia did not know why he was even tolerating rudeness from a man not much more knowledgeable than an ape. Perhaps he realised Shaazia's fragile state and their shared experience of the sperm aspiration made it necessary for him to tolerate her rude husband.

Shaazia watched as he composed himself. 'I believe that your wife might be suffering from endometriosis. We will do the laparoscopy to understand what could be happening within her uterus. We will laser out the endometriosis, and then you can try to conceive naturally for six months. If Mrs Abdul does not conceive during those months, we will then discuss further options.'

Dr Selvin placed the pencil on the desk, and it tumbled over before finding a comfortable spot to rest.

'These are avenues you will need to explore, if of course you want a child,' he said softly, as though afraid Mr Abdul would lash out again. 'You could opt for a life without children. There are many couples who choose that path.'

'If it's Allah's will,' Mr Abdul said.

'No.' Shaazia shook her head. 'I want a baby. That is why we are here.' Her head remained bent. She wrung her hands in her lap as though to escape the frustration that raged within her. 'I need a baby to complete me...' Shaazia paused, her voice trembling with pouring tears. 'I am not a good wife. I have to give you a baby from me. I have to be worthy of our marriage.' Shaazia's words were filled with anguish. 'I need to prove my worth...'

'Shaazia!' Mr Abdul yelled. 'You have spoken too much!'

'I'm sorry.' A quiver spread through her. 'Dr Selvin can help us. He's a specialist,' she pleaded. Wiping her eyes with her gloved hands, Shaazia stared at Mr Abdul unhappily as she continued, 'I need a cure for all my ailments.' Her voice oozed desolation. 'Please, Doctor...'

'Oh, Mrs Abdul.' Dr Selvin had focused his gaze on the pencil he had picked up again. 'The pain, infertility... It all sounds like endometriosis to me.'

For a long moment, there was silence.

'Right,' Mr Abdul said at last. 'We will make the appointment for the laparoscopy, and we will take it from there.' Mr Abdul attempted a smile of courtesy as he rose from the chair. Before Shaazia closed the door behind her, she glanced at Dr Selvin and smiled. Her soul felt a moment of calm.

The patients in the waiting room remained aloof, and busied themselves with their laptops and cellphones. The awkwardness in the room matched the feelings within Shaazia. When she spotted her almost seventy-year-old mother-in-law, her heart tightened with anxiety. This woman, with her oval-shaped face, wrinkled skin, and plumped form, was glaring at a mixed-race couple sitting close by.

'Ma,' she called out, and as the woman turned, Shaazia saw her face grow darker, a vein on her forehead pumping.

'Shaazia, what did the doctor say? Yaaseen went out for a smoke. He said that I must ask you.'

'Ma, Dr Selvin says that they need to do a laparoscopy to determine the cause of my not conceiving.' Shaazia looked at her shoes in embarrassment.

'Okay, so there is something wrong with you,' Mrs Abdul replied in a know-it-all tone. 'Before the operation, try the eggs. Mumtaz can't be wrong. That Hakeem helped her.'

Shaazia turned to the reception desk. 'Ma, I want to go for this scope. Dr Selvin is confident that he can assist us.'

'Shaazia,' Mrs Abdul said as she took hold of Shaazia's gloved hand between her roughened palms. 'These doctors, they just want our money!' She grunted. 'Try the Hakeem. If that doesn't work, you can do the scope.'

Shaazia freed her hand from her mother-in-law's tight grip. 'Ma, I'm going to make an appointment.'

'Shaazia...'

'Ma.' Shaazia turned to Mrs Abdul. 'Dr Selvin said that my age is against me. It's now or never. And Yaaseen has given his consent.'

'Shaazia!' Mrs Abdul's voice rose with anger. Couples turned to look at them. Shaazia shifted uncomfortably.

She refused to let down her guard. The older woman could do nothing to her in the presence of all these strangers. Shaazia had decided a few weeks before that she would follow the fertility specialist's recommendation, no matter the cost. She was determined to birth a child from within her own body. Shaazia knew that at home, within the confines of four walls, she would pay her penance.

***

'She's waking up,' a stranger purred. Shaazia had undergone a laparoscopy. After the anaesthesia and hours of restful sleep, which came with exhaustion and stress, anxiety still riddled her nerves; in her haste to hear Dr Selvin's diagnosis, she nibbled at the inside of her lip.

On her awakening, bustling reigned, for the clinic was soon to close. A nurse handed her a sandwich and a cup of tea. Then they removed the catheter, handed her a measuring jug, and told her to urinate in it. Shaazia was embarrassed when the liquid refused to leave her. Mrs Doyle, the appointed nurse on duty, was given the task of handing glasses of water through a crack in the door to Shaazia to 'push the pee' out. After collecting a few drops in the plastic jug, Shaazia was shown back to her bed. She found her husband sitting there with his head lowered, staring at the screen of his cellphone. He did not acknowledge her.

The nurse closed the curtains. 'Mrs Abdul, Dr Selvin would have wanted to speak to you, but he has left. He said to tell you that he has lasered out fourth-stage endometriosis from both your ovaries,' Mrs Doyle explained to them from outside the closed curtain.

'Sister, what does that mean?' Shaazia pulled open the curtains. 'What is the next step?'

Taking in Shaazia's fully covered form, Sister Doyle replied in a brusque tone, 'The endometriosis was very bad and was preventing you from conceiving. You can now try naturally to conceive.' Then in a much gentler tone, she added, 'And if it still doesn't happen, I would advise you to do IVF.'

Shaazia did not miss the look of doubt. 'Is there nothing else wrong?' When Shaazia glanced in her husband's direction, she noticed Sister Doyle's gaze of pity for her.

'It's only the endometriosis which will remain clear for six months. After the six months, it will begin to grow back.'

'What exactly are you saying?' Mr Abdul asked tersely.

'Simply that the endometriosis has prevented your wife from conceiving a child to date,' she explained. 'You have six months to try naturally. Then the endometriosis grows back, and you may need to consider IVF. The decision is entirely yours, of course.'

Amid the scuttle and cleaning before day end, Shaazia was surprised to learn that there were no wheelchairs available to take her to the car.

'Mr Abdul, kindly bring the car to the entrance,' Mrs Doyle said hurriedly. 'I will assist your wife to the car.'

'Nurse, will you so kindly bring her all the way to the car,' said Mr Abdul.

'I will,' Mrs Doyle promised, as she gently took Shaazia's hand in her own.

Mrs Doyle was a short, petite woman who clearly preferred to handle matters personally. Her white uniform sat snugly over her narrow hips, reaching over her beige stocking-covered legs, cascading down into black patent-leather buckled shoes. Shaazia admired the gold epaulettes that the older lady wore on the shoulders of her white uniform. Suddenly, she was all too aware of the reality of her situation. How abnormal her marriage must look to this woman. She, having undergone an operation to cure her infertility to conceive a child from her own womb, with a man who treated her like an illness to remain aloof from.

Shaazia clutched her small bag of cosmetics. As Mrs Doyle neared her, she lagged behind, as though to protect herself from the scrutiny of this older woman.

Then she turned, and a feeling of warmth released inside Shaazia. She searched the older woman's eyes and discovered deep pools of compassion. Shaazia began to weep, and between the tears, words flowed like a river gushing in full stream. 'I really want to conceive a child. We have been trying, but I am struggling to fall pregnant. As Muslim women, having children is expected of us. I know that a child will heal my marriage!'

Mrs Doyle listened carefully to Shaazia before nodding and turning to Mr Abdul, who stood with his hand on the handle of the car door, keeping it ajar.

Mrs Doyle explained that Dr Selvin emphasised the need for a stress-free, calm, and loving environment for patients who suffered from endometriosis. Shaazia would need to feel loved to be able to conceive naturally.

So, Shaazia with her sparkling clean uterus and her dreams of conceiving a child from her own womb, followed her husband, who had nodded as if persuaded by the nurse's recommendations.

The May air was cold and airy, and added mercilessly to the remote overtone which hung frosty and numbing around them. The music from the radio, the smell of stale cigarette smoke, and the light-headedness Shaazia felt post-anaesthesia, were stifling and blurry, and they sank deep into her subconscious, like the red blood which oozed out of her wound, staining her clothes.

***

'It's unbelievable how quickly the time has disappeared in a bat of an eye,' remarked Shaazia as she regarded Mr Abdul. He was seated beneath a duvet in bed, puffing on his pipe as she towel-dried her damp skin, then wrapped the towel tightly around her. She returned to the bathroom to pull on her satin pyjamas, cleanse her face, and brush out her long hair – her nightly routine.

Six months had ended; the endometriosis would begin its rapid growth again. To Shaazia, this was a terrible realisation, because it meant that they had failed to conceive a child naturally. She removed her makeup before applying a cleanser. She wiped off the cleanser with cotton wool and applied a gentle mask, as a special treat for her skin. Besides, she needed a mood booster. Shaazia ensured that the residue from the mask had been washed clean before she applied a generous amount of moisturiser. She then applied kohl to her eyes and deep red lipstick to her lips. There were too many nights when she dressed to seduce the man she was married to.

'So what?' Mr Abdul's retort caused Shaazia to sidestep into the leg of the Elizabethan-style dresser, startled by the detachment in his voice.

'We will just call it quits for a while, and if it happens, it will. If not, surely Allah has a bigger plan.'

'Really, Yaaseen! Do you not see my need for a child?'

Shaazia's reminder brought a small shrug from Mr Abdul's shoulders. 'Allah gives to those who He chooses to,' he responded in a matter-of-fact tone. 'We will get only that which is written out for us. If a baby is not on the cards, then nothing can make it happen.' He sucked onto his pipe and released wisps of smoke into the air.

Shaazia opened her mouth to reply, but Mr Abdul's indifference to her feelings made her choose not to. Her husband's apathetic attitude had stolen her sexual appetite.

Sleep did not come easily to Shaazia. The hot Jozi night made her clammy and agitated. Outside, she could hear the moths bumping into closed windows and the crickets beating their legs in annoying screeching. It was one of those nights when sleeping beneath a ceiling fan would have been a welcoming lullaby.

Shaazia was still angered by her husband's words, but in her heart, she knew he was right. Her womb was barren, and she would have to accept her fate.

Shaazia rose from the bed and made her way to the kitchen. Nibbling on a cupcake and sipping on a mug of hot tea, she headed to the lounge. The hot tea burnt her tongue, and she gasped. Fresh tears escaped her eyes, even though she had involuntarily clenched them shut. Slowly, Shaazia settled into the sofa and gathered a soft blanket over her. All the while, silent tears fell from her eyes.

***

It was her absence from their bed that woke Mr Abdul. He sat up and listened. Her sobbing drew and held his attention.

Annoyed, he was drawn towards that rhythmic sound of her heaving between sobs. He made his way towards the sound, holding his cellphone torch in his hand to light his path.

When he saw her, waves of guilt swiftly surged through him, leaving him raw with deep sympathy. No caring husband would ever allow his betrothed to suffer like this. And yet the urge to escape captured him, and he turned away from her.

Mr Abdul swung around at the sound of the mug crashing on the bare tiles. He widened his eyes in shock when he met Shaazia's tired gaze. She turned away quickly, probably not wanting him to know her anguish.

For a few seconds, the world stood still, and then the rapid fluttering of wings of a moth hidden beneath the lit lampshade broke the silence. They both turned to look at the shadow dancing in the glow of the masked lamp.

'Are you all right?' Mr Abdul's words were smothered in distress.

'P-please go… L-leave me alone,' Shaazia stammered.

Mr Abdul made no move to leave. Instead, his eyes lingered on her full, red-painted lips. 'I am so sorry,' he muttered softly, without taking his eyes off her. He stepped forward. Gently, he leaned over her and gathered her in his arms.

'Undress,' he ordered, his voice hoarse with unspoken passion.

'No!' Shaazia cried out.

He groaned like an injured deer, then moved away quickly and stood up.

'Shaazia, look at me.' He spoke gently, lifted her chin, and was startled to see the emptiness in them. His heart mellowed with the sadness of loss. 'We will try the IVF, okay.'

He then turned away and left the room.

***

Shaazia was elated when they reached home. She sat on her bed, just breathing slowly, not daring to move until she felt more at ease. When would her body show signs of change? Had the embryo settled within her uterus? Would she feel the embryo growing? Shaazia stared at her reflection in the mirror: how different she had felt yesterday!

When Yaaseen had first suggested that they try IVF, she had made an appointment to discuss the process with Dr Selvin and to make the necessary arrangements. Dr Selvin explained that fertility drugs would need to be injected into her stomach to stimulate the ovaries to mature a dozen or more eggs for retrieval. The process sounded laborious, and Shaazia, like Mr Abdul, hated thinking about the effort that they would need to put in. They decided to try the Hakeem's offering first, which her mother-in-law had suggested.

When the Hakeem's treatment had failed, Shaazia had plucked up the courage to ask Yaaseen if they could attempt a round of IVF. Permission was granted like a stamp of approval onto a passport for entry into a futuristic world.

Shaazia was thrilled, although she was aware of the gossip that went around – that she had resorted to IVF because her womb was barren. But she ignored the gossip, and eventually it died down.

Shaazia turned the IVF process into a manageable affair for herself and Yaaseen. After learning the intricate art of filling the syringe with the hormone-inducing medication, she injected herself daily. A large portion of the day was set aside for prayer, and she kept her prayer mat in a secluded place in her bedroom, so that she could sit alone in deep meditation and relaxation. They shared the house with her mother-in-law and three sisters-in-law, and because of the chaos that the large family might cause, Mr Abdul had a gate installed to divide the house in two, allowing her some privacy.

Shaazia sighed in contentment as she took in the events of the previous months. Did her husband know the extent of her desire to own this baby? He didn't care about her needs, and the thought brought tears to her eyes and an ache to her ageing heart.

'What is the matter with you, Shaazia Abdul?' she reprimanded herself. 'He doesn't really understand you, but he has paid for a very expensive session of IVF, and for that you should show gratitude.' Besides, she was certain that the baby would bring healing to their marriage.

Warmth spread through her.

Her mother-in-law's voice interrupted her reverie. 'Shaazia, Salma is preparing lunch. Please go help her.'

Shaazia slowly stood up and went to her mother-in-law. She hugged Mrs Abdul, wanting to show appreciation that the older woman had been so accommodating of her recent mood swings.

'Why, Shaazia, it's way past lunchtime, and your husband hasn't eaten.' Mrs Abdul felt her daughter-in-law's hot cheeks and saw the happiness in her eyes. 'How did the process go?'

'Good, with your duahs!' Shaazia wrapped a scarf around her sleek hair. 'Dr Selvin is happy with the embryo transfer. Now we must wait two weeks and make lots of duah,' she pleaded, her earlier feelings of happiness dissipating.

'I will make duah, but Allah knows best,' Mrs Abdul retorted. 'IVF is not of the Quraan. It's tampering with science. If Allah wants you to have a child, He will.'

Shaazia's heart lurched. She stared at her mother-in-law with dismay. 'Please, Ma, your duahs will be accepted. Please.'

Mrs Abdul turned away from her. 'Whatever happens, there must be only good in it.'

Shaazia dropped her hands from her scarf, and she leaned forward to kiss her mother-in-law on the cheek, as was customary for her. 'Shukran, Ma. Then I will definitely conceive this time, Aameen!'

'Don't be so certain, Shaazia.' Mrs Abdul moved away abruptly. 'There is a solution, though. My brother Anver has requested that we accept Fatima into our house as a second wife. Her children will be yours.'

'What?' Her mother-in-law's announcement cut into her like a sharp knife slicing into tough steak.

'Bheti, there will be good in it, you will see,' Mrs Abdul crowed. Her voice bubbled with a know-it-all attitude.

Enraged, Shaazia turned to her mother-in-law. 'Please, Ma, I am not going to share my husband with another woman just because we cannot have children and her father thinks that she will be the suitable surrogate!'

'Shaazia...' Mrs Abdul began, and immediately Shaazia knew what the older woman was going to say. Mrs Abdul was going to revert to her usual counsel: that Shaazia was not getting any younger, that their marriage was not producing children, and that her son needed progeny. Her mother-in-law was correct in everything that she had spelt out, but surely there was hope this time...

Resentment and sadness made Shaazia's voice tremble. 'Ma, you are killing my marriage...'

The transformation in Mrs Abdul's face from egotism to surprise motivated Shaazia to continue. 'You do not see my need to give your son a child! You do not support us!' She threw her hands up in exasperation. 'Whether Islam dictates it or not, I will not allow my husband to take on a second wife!'

'What in Allah's name is going on in here?'

Both Shaazia and Mrs Abdul turned, stunned. They had not noticed Mr Abdul enter the bedroom. Both wife and mother stared at him – with caution.

'What is this blather I hear about you dictating my future?' he demanded, stepping in front of them.

'Please tell Ma to pray for us!' Shaazia moved closer to her husband.

'My son...'

'Ma, please, not now.' He put his hand up to silence her.

Shaazia read the hurt in her mother-in-law's eyes before Mrs Abdul turned to flee from the bedroom. It lifted her spirits to know that her husband had stood in her defence.

That night was sleepless. The ache in Shaazia's heart remained dull and throbbing. Thoughts of Mr Abdul with another woman conquered her thoughts. Her body ached for the feeling of him, but she worried that lovemaking might hinder the procedure. All she could do was wait and see what her body would do with the embryo it had received only a few hours prior.

A few days later, Mrs Abdul broached the topic of the proposal again. Since Yaaseen was away at work, Mrs Abdul informed her daughter-in-law that her son would abide by her wishes this time, especially since they so desperately wanted a child.

'If the IVF doesn't work, then I don't see a problem in accepting Fatima into this house.' She smiled scornfully at Shaazia. 'Perhaps when there are children running around, you will see the wisdom in the arrangement.'

Dumbfounded by Mrs Abdul's confrontation, Shaazia replied, 'And then I will leave this house.'

'I will hold you to your word,' the older woman replied.

Shaazia closed her eyes against her mother-in-law's mocking sneer. Drawing a deep breath, Shaazia straightened her shoulders and walked away. How dare her mother-in-law threaten her? What about her nikaah to her son? Hot tears oozed from her eyes, and she allowed them to fall. She succumbed to the pain that pierced at her heart. Drawing another deep breath, Shaazia decided that she would go to her parents' home to wait out the two weeks.

Shaazia dared not tell her father of the ill treatment she had received; she was terrified of his reaction should he discover that her marriage was rocky.

Shaazia was not able to call her husband to explain her need to visit her parents' home. Usually healthy, that night she became terribly ill. She developed a high fever, and kept drifting in an out of consciousness, talking incoherently of her mother-in-law, which only caused more concern and confusion for her father.

Wracked with worry, her father had called his son-in-law, who did not take the call.

After two weeks of constant caring, worrying, and praying, Shaazia's fever slowly left her, and her father was relieved. However, Shaazia looked thin and drawn; she had lost weight, and her eyes had lost their lustre, leaving her with a sad, haunted look. Mr Fakir had realised, through Shaazia's ramblings, that his once-lively daughter had been hurt, and that something was worrying her. Mr Fakir was afraid of discovering the truth, for only Allah knew what the outcome would be.

Knowing that she could not stay with her father forever, Shaazia returned home when she felt a little stronger accompanied by her mother. Yaaseen met them in the kitchen as he was leaving for work. Shaazia loosened her scarf and reached for him. Her secret, the one she held in her belly, the news she was waiting to share, flooded her with excitement.

'Shaazia, where did you run off to?' Yaaseen's anger tore at her gut. He stood his ground in front of her and placed his hands on his hips, observing them.

Shaazia glared at her husband. Embarrassed by his tone – embarrassed that her mother stood witness to his anger.

'I don't want to hear anything negative said about my mother,' Mr Abdul warned, lifting his hand to silence her. 'You have brought shame to me and Mummy by running away to your father. You actually had the audacity to get him to call me. I didn't take his call. I wasn't in the mood for his counsel on our marriage! And look at you, standing here so innocently. You have wasted forty grand of my hard-earned money with your reckless behaviour.'

Shaazia stared, bewildered by her husband. 'Yaaseen!' she cried desperately, but Mr Abdul continued to speak as though he had not been interrupted.

'Return to your father's house. This marriage is not working out.'

'Yaaseen, please listen to me!' Shaazia grabbed hold of him.

He pushed her, and she fell to the floor. Her mother gasped.

'I divorce you! I give you talaaq!' he shouted.

She couldn't hear what else was being said, but she could hear her own heartbeat, and over it she imagined her mother pleading for mercy. Dense beads of perspiration were expelled from her. Nausea overcame her. She felt fearful for the baby growing inside her. She leaned forward, her body heavy on the ground, letting out the breath she had been holding. Realisation hit her. Her marriage was no longer. It lay like the remains of a bird's nest, in pieces. She would need to remain in seclusion, in her parents' home until the birth of their baby. She would then suckle the infant, and then at the age of two, she would wean him off her breast. It would only be then that she would see Yaaseen again. He would come to her, accompanied by his mother, to lay claim to her most treasured possession. She was well versed in the repercussions of Islamic marriage.

Yaaseen would use his Islamic rights to steal their baby from her.

A Play of Power

Riza Jina didn't live in Lenasia – unlike his future father-in-law, the man they called Bhajee. The man with the perfect white teeth and small straight stature, the grand owner of Lenasia Real Estate, who knew, by virtue of his profession, every street, avenue, house, and shopping centre in the entire Lenasia sprawl. The man who knew who would move out when, how many rooms each house had, how many people could be housed where: Bhajee with his dashing smile and ever-so-charming personality, dared to create an empire large enough to control real estate in the whole of Lenasia and beyond. Somehow, he was even able to create a vision of Riza Jina, the son of the father from that township by the railway, the child who hadn't been back to Lenasia since he was four. Bhajee's ability to create an image of the returning man only went to show his need to know everything estate-related.

The thirty-year-old Riza Jina, the boy who had put in a request to rent property, had been born into the hands of doctors Seedat, Asvat, and Timol who serviced the 'file factory' on one of the many similar streets in Lenasia. Wherever you went in Lenasia you saw narrow streets barren of vegetation and decorated with scattered trash. If you entered Lenasia from the N12 highway, the first thing you saw was swampy wetland merging at car sale rooms on the periphery of a shopping mall. A little further on, on the way to Lenasia South, on the left, there was the Ahmed Kathrada Private Hospital. And at the intersection, before Trade Route Mall, when you took a right turn at the traffic lights, you followed the route down a long road called Nirvana Drive which divided Lenasia from Extension 13. Then there was the railway station, home to waiting taxis and hawkers, which served as the gateway to the business distinct termed 'Top Shops' – the area where it was cheap to buy Indian groceries, fruit and vegetables, material, and more.

It was in this township, that Bhajee, as behoved a model estate agent, had ordered a house to be built, a house with four flats big enough to house his progeny, their spouses, and children. This was also the township in which he proposed, in exchange for free rental, that Riza Jina would marry his daughter Kauthar, a spinster growing older through the years. Riza accepted this benefiting proposition with a short but sweet, all-purpose Insh'Allah.

Nobody in Lenasia dared to believe it. 'What? Riza Jina's going to marry her, Bhajee's spinster daughter?' But three months later, Bhajee handed over the keys to his new son-in-law, and Riza Jina was duly married to the estate tycoon's daughter.

After the wedding, Riza moved into the house at number 66 Amber Street, where he entered a different world. Within days, he'd made the wonderful discovery that his youth had been spent doing harsh labour. Riza and Kauthar enjoyed a honeymoon in Mauritius and an annual trip to Switzerland – to check on the investments abroad. This lifting of the veil – the reality his friends had joked about – uplifted Riza so much that a seed of happiness was sown. This seed, born of money squandering and partying, was to be a golden gift horse that delivered him from doing any labour, into a life of early retirement.

***

On that day, a full decade and four granddaughters later, the electricity supply at 66 Amber Street ceased. Bhajee experienced a rare moment of darkness in his heart.

The gushing of a water pump churning clogged, and the rhythmic motion of the fridge motor beating in its cage, stopped. The rapid movement of colour disappeared off the television set, dissolving the display into starry black. Something had disturbed the power flow. The electricity at 66 Amber Street had been cut.

Silence reigned for only a few seconds, and then the house woke to a sudden spark of life like a car's rusty engine – loud and aggressive. The children were eager to announce the news. "The television is not working!" They were equally eager to dish out instructions. "Check if the neighbours have electricity!" The other homes in their neighbourhood had electricity. Their neighbourhood WhatsApp group remained silent, which made the problem an isolated case – one which the occupants at 66 Amber Street would need to sort out. Bhajee did not understand the reason for the electricity cut when his meter had been neatly bypassed a good six years earlier, by thieves who had stolen the meter, thereby gifting 66 Amber Street with a free supply of electricity.

Mrs S, the housekeeper, became frantic. The cakes that she had, moments before, placed in the oven would surely cave in and form molten volcano holes. After a frantic search for paper and the pen she had hidden from the children but had forgotten where, Mrs S made the expected call to City Power and hung on, listening to the tune of Mozart's melody in eager anticipation to speak to the 'next available consultant'. The process dragged on. She sat on a small cushioned stool embroidered in gold thread, with the handset cradled in her right hand against her ear.

The children needed to be ferried to extramurals. Their driver, Uncle Eric, ran around, heaving in and then sighing out loud. The usual. Today it was all a tad bit quieter without the rhythmic grind of moving electricity. The wooden door leading to the garage was hurriedly opened and then shut, closing the youngest child, a toddler, away from the forbidden danger lurking in the darkened space which daily housed four vehicles. Uncle Eric carried a plastic stool into the garage and placed it in the small space between the garage door and the car. Duly elevated, he was able to reach and pull on the rope which hung on the edge of a plastic block, above his head. The garage door refused to budge into manual control. Uncle Eric then hurried back into the house and ushered the four little girls out through the front door. On his way out, he left the car keys next to the telephone on the small antique coffee table. The risks of getting mugged were high. It was not safe walking the short route from

Amber Street to the swimming pool at 166 Pine Avenue. Uncle Eric carried the toddler and held on firmly to the hand of the four-year-old. The six- and the eight-year-old walked with them. The children shouted out their greetings to Mrs S, who still hung on to her handset, the outstretched cord bouncing in recurring waves, back and forth, back and forth.

It was already too much to handle. Only a full nineteen minutes without electricity. The residents at 66 Amber Street expected the electricity to return like a loyal dog coming home, but there was nothing. City Power logged the fault and promised to send out technicians who did not come as promised, and the minutes rolled on into hours. Uncle Eric walked to collect the children from swimming lessons. Mrs S heated the food on the gas stove and served it to the family amid shadows from dancing candle flames. She then got the children ready for bed and lay with them in the dark, fending off the monsters that lurked in the night. She left the room only when they entered dreamland.

The technicians did not come, and the night rolled mercilessly into day. At daybreak, Mrs S placed yet another call to City Power and was told that the technicians had come, sometime during the night. Number 66 Amber Street had not seen them because the house still wore signs of darkness during the early parts of the morning when the occupants rose for their meal before the day's activities. The children spotted the ajar door on the small green electricity box positioned on the municipal boundary of their opposite neighbour's house. On further investigation with their grandfather, the children anxiously reported to Mrs S that the meter had been stolen. Bhajee grimaced – the meter had been stolen years ago. What could possibly have happened now?

A third call was placed to City Power, and after yet another day of waiting, a solo technician arrived at 66 Amber Street. The children watched the sun melt across the horizon in a spiral of red and orange streaks. The call of prayer sounded across from one mosque to the other. The technician confirmed the theft and advised that the meter be reported stolen. There was absolutely *nothing* that he could do further. Without further ado, darkness once again cascaded on the house at 66 Amber

Street. Twenty-six hours of no electricity. And counting!

'Come now,' Bhajee pleaded. 'Is there nothing that can be done for us?'

'No.' The technician smirked.

'Come, we walk.' Bhajee chased his granddaughters back into the house and closed the door to their pleas. He went with the technician to his white van.

'Will one hundred rands be okay?' He opened his wallet just enough to allow the technician to survey the wads of cash sandwiched between the leather. The technician stared on, his face showing no emotion.

'Two hundred?' Bhajee reached out for the technician's hand and placed the orange note on his palm.

The technician shoved the note into his pocket then crossed the road to the green electricity box. He played with the wires on the board for what seemed like two short minutes – the time it takes for the sand to spill through the sand timer as you brush your teeth. Number 66 Amber Street rose to the occasion. A bribe offered. A bribe accepted. And, then there was light. It was all too easy. The prepaid meter had been bypassed for an orange note bearing a print of a leopard.

'Report the meter stolen. Tomorrow your electricity will be cut again. Sort out the meter,' the technician called out before driving off.

No sooner had the door closed that Bhajee put out a call to all his friends owing him favours. The councillors of Lenasia also needed to know – he placed a call to the direct lines of the ANC and the DA councillor. They explained that he would have to personally report the stolen meter at the police station and then go to City Power with his pre-paid electricity receipts to get a new meter fitted in. This was too much for Bhajee to handle. He was fighting against this unknown life, which was very new yet had subsumed everything – his home, his energy, and his every second of peace. Hour in and hour out – the complaints from the children, the manual control of the garage doors, and the constant worry of the consequences of not reporting the stolen meter all those years ago penetrated deep into his subconscious.

***

Riza accepted Bhajee's call just as his tanned skin was being rubbed with a delicate concoction of aromatherapy oils. He waved his hand at the therapist, motioning for her to switch off the sweet melody on the sound system. The beautiful young therapist lifted the lowered neckline of her starched white uniform which had minutes earlier exposed rather a lot of desirable flesh to her best-paying client. She left the room. He rose and sat upright on the edge of the massage bed, his lower body loosely wrapped in a white towel.

'Yes, Dad, sorry. The TV was on. You were saying?'

'Riza, Riza! Leave the Swish accounts. I vill tell Nicholash to send me report. Pleash just come home. There's tragedy, big problems!' Bhajee scrambled through his words, mushing them in his haste.

'Dad, slow down! I can barely hear what you're saying!' Riza could not hide his annoyance. His massage with his Swiss goddess had been rudely interrupted.

'Don't be smart with me, boy! Return home at once.' The line went dead. Riza sighed.

He would wait to see if Kauthar had received a call from her father. Until then, he had more pressing issues to attend to. He laughed and rubbed a hand through his hair, fluffing it out on the top. He rang the bell, and the therapist returned and locked the door behind her.

Hours later, Riza Jina met a hysterical Kauthar in the hotel lobby.

'Riza where were you?' Her stare was bewildered, her usually straight hair standing in curls on top of her head. Her red eyes held smudges of old mascara. It was 3pm, and she still wore satin pyjamas with creased lines.

'I called you a million times! Daddy called! Something has happened to the children... It must be Leeyana. I know we should have brought her with...'

Riza went to her and held her while slowly pushing her backwards into the hotel room. Kauthar was making a scene, and Riza could not deal with her outburst. He needed to maintain the image he had created for himself.

'Darling, I was with Nicholas. We had arranged an early appointment to discuss the portfolio,' he softly murmured into her hair, still holding her.

'Don't fuck with me Riza! And don't touch me! I called Nicholas, and he hadn't heard from you! Just book the damn flights, and let's go home!'

Riza knew better than to further anger his wife, so he put a quick call to the airlines and booked a one-night stopover in Dubai before returning home. He had to collect a box of cigars for his good friend Mahesh. He would deal with Kauthar's rage later.

***

At the bottom of the globe, in the township of Lenasia, 66 Amber Street was once again shrouded in darkness. The technician had kept his word and switched off the electricity. The children whined and complained. 'What is there to do? There's no Netflix!'

Mrs S was back on duty, and her ploy of using the television to babysit the children would no longer work, since there was no electricity. She hired a carpenter to build a zip line in the garden to entertain the children. An arrangement was made with the neighbours at a cost of one thousand rand to run an extension cord from their power point into the garden at 66 Amber Street.

Bhajee was at his wits' end. He couldn't produce prepaid electricity receipts for the six years during which 66 Amber Street had basked in light for free. He placed further calls to all his friends who owed him favours, but to no avail. Allah wanted him to pay penance for his debts. When the freezers started pouring water on the wooden flooring, he sent Uncle Eric to purchase a generator. These were costly gadgets as they used petrol, and with the high cost of fuel, Bhajee, too, had resorted to walking to mosque. Fitting the generator with the switch had also cost him a small fortune, but these were desperate times, and so he reluctantly signed the cheques.

Bhajee felt assurance knowing that his daughter and son-in-law were returning home within a day. Then the feelings of happiness changed to anguish when news of the flights being delayed reached him. The residents at 66 Amber Street were five days and counting without electricity. The moods were tipping over into aggression.

Exasperated, Bhajee went in search of the pre-paid meter receipts, frustrated by his own abandonment of his office since retirement, which caused him to offer up profanities. It reduced him wondering what had possessed him to allow Riza full control of his dynasty. He refused to leave his office, and seated at his desk, he packed, filed, and only once he found a shoe box containing the payment receipts, did he retire to bed. By the next morning the task ahead seemed less frightening and almost forgiving. He began to enjoy the first moments of waking to a darkened space, having to figure out how things worked: the art of lighting a gas stove and the mastery of starting up the generator.

***

Much to his chagrin, Bhajee, accompanied by Uncle Eric, went to City Power to plead his case. Uncle Eric was a bad driver, nervous and anxious, and when he took his eyes off the road to look over his shoulder, Bhajee stressed. Uncle Eric straddled the lanes, his wing mirrors only millimetres away from scraping the cars alongside, and Bhajee found it nauseating to watch cars swerve away from them, blasting their horns as they moved. Without realising it, Uncle Eric had given Bhajee a reason to drive again, reuniting him with the textures of mid-afternoon Jozi traffic and the feeling of control and mastery when he could easily hash lanes to reach his destination.

Uncle Eric parked outside the municipal building, scratching the tyre rims on the pavement. Men and women streamed through the open doors, carrying bags and folders of paper, striding to the room that contained the City Power officials. By now, Uncle Eric had hurried on ahead of Bhajee, who was unhappy that he couldn't keep up. Uncle Eric glanced back, checking to see if the older man was coping climbing up the steps, and paused when Bhajee stopped against the railing to catch his breath. At the entrance to the City Power office, people stepped forward to occupy the empty seats among rows of occupied ones. Bhajee was annoyed when all the chairs were taken and that nobody had risen to offer him a seat. An official motioned for him to stand with the others in a row, waiting for the chain of people to move along. Four desks with officials sitting behind them, served four persons at a given time, which meant that soon there would be empty chairs waiting for occupants to sit in them. But Bhajee was already highly irritated after his tiresome arrival and refused to follow the official's direction.

'It's okay,' he persisted. 'I will wait here.'

But the official, with the name of Mr Modau, shook his head and moved forward. He hunched his shoulders and pointed to the desks at the front, then beckoned to Bhajee to join him. Bhajee followed him past the rows of chairs to the front where the other officials sat. Several people rose and pushed forward with them, the steel chair legs grinding against the bare floor. Two women, dressed in long, blue-printed shweshwe dresses, shouted out, complaining that they were waiting, and Bhajee should, too. Mr Modau grew into something manly and tough in their wake, instructing them to remain seated, his voice melting into gentle monosyllables.

Mr Modau led Bhajee to a narrow passage, sneezing and grunting as they made their way past two closed rooms with tinted windows. Mr Modau pushed open the door to the third room, and Bhajee was surprised to find himself entering a large room with a big mahogany-fashioned desk, a computer screen, and a rotating leather-upholstered chair. Bhajee was suddenly frightened. *How does one explain that the thieves had gifted him free electricity for six years? What now? What would the penalty be?*

Mr Modau was kind and friendly. Bhajee suspected that he was in a junior position. He was surprised later to learn that he was the senior manager, but equally unsurprised to discover that he was new at this centre. His attention and interest made Bhajee relax with him – to the point where he disclosed everything about his pressing issue and moved closer to him, pleading with him to have mercy on his case.

On reaching the end of his story, Bhajee was surprised when Mr Modau reached his hands to him, and shocked when he held his hand sandwiched between his two, cradling them with respect the way one would when greeting an older person.

'Let's see what we can do,' Mr Modau said, smiling.

Watching him turn to his computer screen to switch it on, Bhajee was sure that everything would turn out well.

'Where are the pre-paid receipts?' he asked.

'I have them all here.' Bhajee placed a purple plastic folder in front of Mr Modau, who then turned to his computer and pulled his chair forward to the table. He scanned the folder of slips and then with his index finger pressed at the letters on the keyboard.

'Hmm, let's see. Are you Ka Ching Ching?'

'Me?' Bhajee looked over Mr Modau's shoulder.

'Yes, Umnumzana. This account belongs to Ka Ching Ching.'

'Young man, are you trying to be funny?' Bhajee rebuked. 'Do I look Chinese?'

'I'm sorry sir,' Mr Modau replied, 'but this account is not yours.'

'Of course it is mine!'

'See, it says here.' Mr Modau turned the computer to face Bhajee and pressed his index finger to the screen. 'It states here that the owner for the address 66 Amber Street is Ka Ching Ching.'

'That's ridiculous! There are no Chinese in Lenasia!'

Mr Modau turned away from the computer. With long fingers he reached for a pen among others in a tin can on his desk. He scribbled his name and phone number onto the corner of his calendar, tore it off, and placed it in front of Bhajee.

'You have a big problem. Let me see if I can sort it out. You can wait for my call. Thank you.' His smile never left his eyes.

Watching him turn back to face his computer screen, Bhajee gingerly stood up and hobbled out of the office.

'I will really appreciate it if you can assist me, please.'

Mr Modau nodded. However, Bajee was unsure whether he would.

***

The following day, Mr Modau waited for Bhajee in his office, his face neatly shaven, his hair newly trimmed and glossy with shine. He wore tailored grey pants with a starched white shirt, and a deep blue tie with fine white dots that clasped the collar of the shirt.

His dismal expression came as no surprise to Bhajee. He already knew to expect it. When Bhajee had called that morning, defeated by the darkness that still held onto the abode at number 66 Amber Street, Mr Modau's abrupt tone made Bhajee think he'd misconstrued the instruction.

He had not told Bhajee that he need not bother coming in to receive the news that could easily be related on the telephone. Bhajee leaned his heavy head back against the seat, breathing in the musky scent of genuine leather. It all felt nerve-wracking to him. Anxiously, he prayed that this be his last day to endure such torture.

Mr Modau looked as if he'd been working for hours, and greeted Bhajee in a way that instantly made him worry. Mr Modau appeared nervous, and as he settled back into his chair, his face seemed haunted, his manner hurried. He instructed Bhajee to place the plastic folder of the electricity receipts on the table. He was ready to talk business.

Bhajee registered Mr Modau's troubled expression and realised the seriousness of the situation. 'Yes, sir?' he said softly. 'How can you help me?'

Mr Modau recoiled, looking alarmed. 'I am afraid that I cannot help you.' His voice rose shakily. 'You are in arrears of six years of electricity payment. The fine for that is five hundred thousand rands, at least. Your account is not your own. We don't know if your house is your own. So, you stand the risk of having your property repossessed.'

Bhajee's face crumbled into an angry scowl, and he crossed his arms defensively across his chest. 'What!' he whispered. 'That is not possible!'

'According to records, in 2010, when City Power installed the pilot phase of pre-paid meters, they may have fabricated names of the owners, so perhaps that can be sorted out,' Mr Modau explained. 'Pay the money for the arrears payment and then we can get a new meter installed in your name. It will be okay.'

'No, it's not *okay*!' Bhajee lashed out. 'How can it be okay! You want me to pay half a million for something which was out of my control! I will not!'

Bhajee felt pathetic trying to deceive the official, and Mr Modau clearly had little interest in what Bhajee had to say. His eyes remained fixed on Bhajee, judging him, considering an outcome in his head.

Mr Modau got up, beads of sweat glistening on his skin. He clearly wanted nothing more to do with Bhajee. 'Sir, you need to pay what is owed to us. You were well aware, all these years, that you were not paying for electricity.' His voice came out dismissively.

Bhajee stumbled back, reaching clumsily for his walking stick. He looked at Mr Modau with shock, fearful that his reaction might alarm Mr Modau into verbal assault.

As Bhajee and Uncle Eric left the CP offices, the morning sun was bleak, and the streets were fully lit and busy. Cars covered the streets in patterns of colours and models. They weaved through the lanes that twined into the city and onto the M1 South highway, leading back to Lenasia.

Bhajee grunted loudly, clenching the steering wheel. His frown ran deep furrows on his forehead, and he rubbed his red eyes.

'What now?' he asked no one in particular. He had forgotten Uncle Eric, and only at the dramatic blast of a car's horn did he turn to face his passenger, his expression tense.

'What the fuck, Eric? If you knew how to drive, we wouldn't be in this bloody mess!'

Uncle Eric kept staring straight ahead, clearly oblivious to the storm of worry brewing in his employer's thoughts.

***

The days after Bhajee's meeting at City Power were filled with suspense. On the surface, little seemed to have changed.

The generator got switched on during the wee hours of the morning when Mrs S hurried to prepare breakfast and supper for the family. The generator was switched off when Mrs S had completed her chore of vacuuming the house. Then, when the night shadows grew, the sound of a revving engine filled the house once more. To the community, 66 Amber Street was just a house with a meter stolen, nothing wrong or dishonest, nothing treacherous, and nothing to be ashamed of. And yet, after his meeting with Mr Modau, Bhajee had been labelled a thief, one who had stolen something, knowing the consequences.

***

Kauthar's children hugged and kissed her as if she'd been gone for months. Then, remembering their father standing in the doorway, they ran into his tight embrace. Kauthar was moody, and ascended the steps quickly to her father's chambers. In her father's arms, she demanded that he help her seek a divorce from Riza. She gazed into Bhajee's knowing eyes, and everything felt comforting and free. She exclaimed love for her father, words that she had never offered to Riza. There was something warrior -like and avenging about the plan they were embarking on.

'It shouldn't take long,' Bhajee assured his daughter. 'Just a few minutes, and then we can be rid of the scoundrel.'

Later, they stood in counsel together. In a voice sterner than expected, Bhajee addressed them with authority. He spoke to Riza as an angered father might, one who was emotional over his daughter's sadness. No explanation was given. Riza said nothing. He simply stood aloof; his flat expression came as no surprise to Kauthar.

The laughter and playful banter of the children playing in the rooms below filled the passages at number 66 Amber Street.

'Daddy,' Riza interrupted finally, 'do you want me sort out the power outage? I can call up my buddies.'

Kauthar was annoyed with the change that the conversation took.

'Bhajee, allow me to please sort out the electricity. It is the least that I can do... before leaving." Riza persisted. Bhajee looked from his son-in-law to his daughter. Kauthar read the desperation in her father's eyes. Shocked, she realised how vulnerable her father appeared, and she wondered at the immensity of the problem. Only then did she smell the paan on his breath, see the spittle of betel leaf bleeding off the corners of his mouth. A few red stains tainted his usually immaculate attire. 'Eating paan is a lazy man's bad habit,' he had once told her. 'It's something that I will never do.'

'Daddy,' she said. 'Don't worry, Riza will make a plan.'

Riza smiled at her. She ignored him.

'Daddy, give me a few hours.' Riza waved his phone in the air.

The children had gathered in the room, visibly excited by their father's promise that the electricity would soon be restored.

***

In his own chambers, Riza made a call to Mahesh, his friend and partner in crime.

'Hey Boet. Howzit? I'm back. Need a huge favour please.' Riza then explained the plan to Mahesh.

***

Three hours later, when the sky hung like a canvas in soft pinks, and the interior of the house at 66 Amber Street was preparing to welcome the dark, the doorbell rang. Bhajee watched as Mrs S opened the front door, welcoming in Mahesh and a stranger. Bhajee took note of their professional attire. He eyed the briefcase Mahesh carried with curiosity and suspicion.

'Mahesh Bhai, welcome, come sit,' Bhajee said while patting the seat next to him. 'How are you doing?' He ignored the stranger. The man sat down on the sofa across from them.

'Hello, hello Uncle. I'm good, good, and how are you, Uncle?' Mahesh responded.

'You know how it is with us! We getting old. It's arthritis and backache and everything else. How's your dad doing? Still slogging for the Patels?' Bhajee asked.

'Uncle, Dad is okay. I told him to retire now. I will take care of him. There's a deal coming up. We expecting a lot from the returns,' Mahesh replied.

'That's good to hear. Shame, your mum worked hard all these years making papar from early morning. I always told my tenants to buy from her,' retorted Bhajee.

'Yes, thank you, Uncle. They always asked for discount, and Mum gave in because you referred them.'

At this, Bhajee laughed. 'That's Indian mentality, my son, but at least they bought, and you grew big and so jaaroh!'

The stranger cleared his throat. Bhajee ignored the man.

'Mrs S,' he called out. 'Please tell Riza that Mahesh is here, and also tell Eric to start up the generator! It's so damn dark in here!'

Bhajee was surprised to see Mahesh get up. The younger man put out his hand, beckoning Bhajee to the dining room table.

'Uncle, Riza has told me about your electricity problems. Come, we sit and talk.'

He pulled out a chair for the older man. 'I have brought Mr Mahlangu along; he is the best attorney for this job.'

Bhajee sat down and studied the man who took the seat at the head of the table. He was tall, slender, and clean shaved. He was dressed in a black suit with a crisp white shirt and black tie. Mahesh had handed the man the briefcase, and he busied himself retrieving wads of paper which he placed in front of him.

'Mrs S!' Bhajee shouted.

Mrs S entered and carefully set two candles in the centre of the table. She lit them. 'Riza and Eric are gone to fill the generator.'

'Kauthar? Call Kauthar, then.'

'Kauthar has a migraine and is in deep slumber.'

At that moment, Bhajee's phone beeped, and he opened it to retrieve a message from Nicholas, his investment banker.

Take the Deal, the message read.

'Okay, okay, I'm ready for it. Tell me how much must I pay!' Bhajee shouted.

'Hello, sir,' Mr Mahlangu began. 'We can cancel the debt

that you owe City Power. We can also change the name of the account.'

'How much will it cost me? Those bloody chors want half a million rands!'

'We have drawn up the documents for you to read through. Everything needs to be done *legally* this time. We really don't want you to experience further problems.'

Bhajee was aware of the lawyer's emphasis on the word 'legally'. *Has Riza told them about the free electricity they have been running on all these years?*

'Okay! How much? How much?'

'Fifty thousand rands.'

Bhajee exhaled slowly. He was relieved.

'There is one problem, though.' Mr Mahlangu waved a sheet of paper in the air. 'The debt is registered on your name. This means that you will need to sign off the title deeds of this house to Riza. We can't use your daughter's name, as she shares your surname.'

Bhajee's pulse quickened. He felt hot. He was suddenly alert. *Do they think he is stupid! He cannot possibly give everything to Riza! But what choice does he have?*

'We can change everything after. We assure you. After CP is out of the picture.'

Bhajee was uncertain. He wished it were brighter in the room. He was always good at reading people's expressions. He also needed to read through the documents but felt assured that he could go through them the next day. Yes, yes, he could discuss the deal with Kauthar.

'Sir, I must tell you, though. This deal is only valid for the next hour.' Mr Mahlangu was now standing next to him. He bent and put the page down in front of Bhajee. The pen rolled on its edge, a silver Parker pen. The light from the flame reflected off the metallic silver.

'We require you to sign here and here.'

Bhajee needed advice. He picked up his phone and dialled his advisor, Nicholas. The phone went to his answering machine. He sent Nicholas a message that read – *Please call me, need advice.* No response. The minutes ticked on. He weighed his options. *The money isn't much. The change in name? At least they will be rid of that Mr Ka Ching Ching fellow!* He stared at his phone, willing a response. Nothing. The light that emanated from the screen blinded him, and when he looked up, the black spots were still there. Bhajee picked up the pen offered to him and signed.

Defeated, he was barely aware of the two men leaving.

The next morning brought sounds of laughter and happiness – there was Netflix once more. Bhajee watched the smiles on his granddaughters' faces. Mrs S and Uncle Eric were chatting away happily in the kitchen. His daughter Kauthar joined him for breakfast, and when he saw her dishevelled appearance and her tear-stained eyes, he realised he had indeed made a grave mistake. Much to his dismay, Bhajee had lost his dynasty to the philandering hands of his son-in-law, a dynasty worth much more than the money he had owed to City Power.

Farook

Ginger snakes his body between my bare legs and into my arms. His fur is soothing against my unshaven legs. The paperwork falls from my hands onto the tiles, decorating them.

'Silly cat!' I say. 'Now look at what you have done!'

I push him off me and bend to pick up the papers. Ginger again attempts to push into me, rubbing his body into mine in the same way that he does when he wants a snack.

'Not now, Ginger!' I shout.

Ginger doesn't meow, and I think nothing of it. I pick him up and drop him onto the floor at my feet. A drop of blood falls in a crimson smudge onto the invoice in my hand, blocking out the numbers. I feel my heart rate quicken. My palms become sweaty. I'm shocked! My thoughts run wild! I pick him up again, searching frantically for a wound. It is then that I notice something hanging from Ginger's mouth. I watch as he spits the thing at my feet. It moves. It screeches. The small, brown-haired creature is caught in Ginger's hold.

My cat has brought me a gift. A mouse. A live...squirming... hairy mouse!

I scream then – loud, crazy obscenities. Nobody hears me since I live alone. No one will rescue me from this mouse, or the mouse from me. My eyes swell and tears push forward. These days, these moments visit me often. Perhaps it comes with being doomed a spinster. I sniff. There are no tissues, so I use the bottom of my blouse to wipe my nose. The invoices are now stained in brown-and-crimson tattoos, marking my new reality.

In all the drama, Ginger lets go of the mouse, and it dashes into my kitchen. I don't see where it goes. The knocking of my heart slows down, and I regain my usual tired self. Ginger looks up at me. I smile, lift him into my arms, and we settle into the sofa together.

'Thank you, old boy,' I say. 'Thank you for the gift.' He nuzzles his face into mine. The moment allows me to reminisce about a time when I only briefly acknowledged the bills to be paid. And like stepping stones in my mind, other memories grow from that thought, forcing me to remember *him*.

We first met at a mutual friend's one-year-old daughter's birthday party, eating popcorn out of hats, pink melted marshmallows, blue icing on cake. Across the carousel we found that we shared the same interests, lived in the same extension in Lenasia, and enjoyed the same takeout food, Akhalwaya's toasted polony specials. He borrowed a pen from the host to write my number on the back of his arm.

In the beginning, we chatted on the telephone for hours, talking about music and books, the butchery where he worked, the delicious taste of salted green mangos when dried in the December sun. Within weeks, we took each other for long, serene walks around Rose Park, passing balls back to playing children, eating coconut-flavoured milk ice creams off sticks, and ending with shy, quick handshakes. My mother was not happy with him. She always wanted more for me in a marriage partner. She was also not happy that he was Cockney. I didn't care about all of that. How did his village in India really affect my life? Like really! Mother did not understand. She explained that our cultures are different. '"They" prepare their meals differently. "They" talk a different language,' she moaned.

Mother worried that I wouldn't adjust to this new way of living. That he had chosen business over studying was another topic, Mother lamented. 'What would so-and-so say? Ya Allah! I have failed at parenting!' she would wail dramatically. 'My only daughter is infatuated with a man who sells meat!' Mother was more interested in appeasing the Joneses than her own daughter, her own flesh. I once yelled at her; I wanted her to feel all the emotions I was experiencing for this one man, for Farook. I told her that I loved him; I loved him, and I loved the way he made me feel.

During the earlier stages of our courtship, my parents always accompanied us because Mother was concerned that people would gossip, and my reputation would be tarnished for years to come. My parents took me to meet him. He was not allowed home. They seemed enough, those small, casual, and imperfect meetings. It was worth being with him for those few treasured moments at a time. Afterwards, when we separated, we would yearn for each other's existence for just a minute longer.

I never had to endure a samoosa run. The idea frightened me. The endearing formal garment, in pastel shades and head scarf draped with style around my head; clothing designed to attract the heart of the Mr Eligible's mother. At best, I imagined that I would look shy and reserved; at worst I was terrified that my hands might tremble so viciously that in offering the tea, I would topple the tray.

I had managed to avoid it until then; even before Farook, nobody had visited. During those years, I had waited in anticipation and prayer. Each morning, I checked myself in the tall mirror that hung inside the door of mother's cupboard, scrutinising my blemished skin and ponytailed hair. When I tried to brush out my hair and leave it free, Mother would close in around me to plait my hair while saying, 'No, it looks too bushy loose.'

With her domineering personality, straightforwardness, and inclination to make a scene if something angered her, Mother made for a powerful dictator of my dress code and general appearance. I followed her instructions when she pointed out clothes to wear and decisions to be made. Mother was strict, and obeying orders was not something I dared to contest. My mother was part of a generation for whom submissive children, good education, and virtuous reputation meant everything.

My mother, who was the middle child among five siblings, had experienced a childhood being chastised by her older brothers and being nanny to her younger brothers. My mother told me that she often had to fight for that last candy bar. She had later gone to Pakistan to study medicine and returned to South Africa an engaged general practitioner. After a one-year courtship, which saw my father visiting whenever possible, they had married, just weeks before my mother started an internship at Coronation Hospital. My mother had given my father the financial freedom to experiment with various occupations. My father had given my mother the adventure that comes with new experiences. They had, in common, solid religious belief and strong values to educate me and my younger brother, and of course to see us both well married.

And then, after only the second month of courtship, Mother very crudely announced that she had expected that Farook's parents would call to finalise everything. It was the feeling of being in love that excited me, that nourished our relationship and prompted me to speak to Farook about Mother's expectations. The ultimate realisation came in his mother's phone call, hearing my name in the conversation, Mother making arrangements for the meeting, as if I'd always been destined to marry into the Saley family.

On the day of the meeting, we were up at dawn for our early morning prayer. We had a hasty breakfast, during which Mother, who had slept very little during the night, dashed around busily in the kitchen. Then Father, Brother, and I were shifted around our house to allow Aunty Rose the space to clean while Mother dished out instructions. Why was Mother stressing us all out?

She hoisted platters of savouries and others with sweetmeats, delicacies for the meeting, onto the pink-themed set tables. Relying on tales told to her by friends of their daughters' samoosa runs, she moved around like a fly, a frenzied abandon that placed strain on her back and shoulders. Her callousness, so indicative of women who are confident in themselves, received quite a few annoyed glances from Father, which only made me feel more harassed with anticipation.

At last, Mother went for a shower, dressed, and composed herself. Thank goodness that it was just us, and the aunts hadn't come, as originally planned. The house would have been full, with stress and tension stringing in chorus notes. I retired to my own room to dress for the occasion. I settled on wearing a black, ankle-length skirt with a pink jersey. I tied my long hair into a bun and hid it beneath a draped black stretch scarf.

By then, Farook and his mother had arrived, and Mother had undergone a metamorphosis, of sorts. The stressed-out, frowning, fierce woman from earlier was left somewhere, cast off the way a butterfly leaves its cocoon. She had acquired a graceful, almost regal manner. Once more taking up her role of mother, she moved Father and his ashtray to the passage beyond the kitchen and chased Brother into his room. Once more, her domineering command had forced her family to keep to the rules.

When Farook rang the bell, Mother opened the door. A woman followed in his footsteps. She quickened her pace and embraced Mother, greeting in Arabic, 'Asalaamu-alaykum!' Then she changed to English. 'How are you?'

It was Mairoonisha, Farook's mother. After greeting Mother, warmly but quickly, she turned to me, gushing, 'Ah, Farook, is this my daughter-in-law?' She tried to sweep me into her arms, but I resisted her embrace. She seemed to recoil, then recovering her poise, she smiled at me and offered me her hand instead. Mother frowned at me and grimaced, as if my response to Farook's mother had caused her embarrassment.

'Mairoonisha, please come sit.' She motioned gently to the sofa within her reach.

We entered the living room, where the purple flowers of the bougainvillea provided beauty to the room.

Now Farook approached. Mother and Farook embraced, and then abruptly stood apart as if to ease the unspoken thoughts hidden within both. They smiled at each other, but the unease between them was obvious.

'Come, we have tea. Na'eema, go make the tea please,' Mother said.

Earlier, Mother had instructed that I switch off the oven; I had forgotten to do so, and the pies had darkened to a crispy chocolate brown. I was about to remove them when I saw the spread of savouries that had already been set out. Relieved, I realised I didn't have to take out the pies. I hated throwing away food. I would pack them for my work lunch.

Aunty Mairoonisha and Farook helped themselves to the full spread of savouries, chocolate cake, and biscuits, sipped their masala tea and responded warmly to Mother's constant, pleasant chatter. But they kept looking around, as if inspecting for dust. Mother had opened the front door, and the sun, streaming in, lit up the brown oak furniture, brought out the depth of the butter-yellow walls, and even seemed to brighten the muted flower-design tapestry.

Farook and I exchanged the odd word, but we remained guarded in the presence of our mothers. Sensing that we needed to be alone, to overcome our nervousness, Aunty Mairoonisha asked if she could perform the late afternoon prayer. She had made ablution already, and the time had set in.

'Of course,' Mother said.

After another ritual exchange of pleasantries, Mother led Aunty Mairoonisha to my bedroom. The paintings on the wall gave it a radical look that one associated with an artist's studio.

'Isn't this interesting? I never allow Sellotape on my walls.'

'Yes, yes! Na'eema likes to exhibit her art in her space. I allow it.'

Heightened by all the excitement, Farook eagerly began silly prattle, but I felt uncomfortable and excused myself to prepare more boiled tea in the kitchen. As I returned to the dining room, I saw the silhouette of Aunty Mairoonisha with her head on the floor, bent to one side, peering under my bed. I couldn't be sure, but she seemed to be looking for something. Then Mother came up behind her and nudged her burkah-clad back. Aunty Mairoonisha rose to her feet. Mother and Aunty Mairoonisha stood there for a moment, staring at a small box I didn't recognise, lying on the floor; their silence seemed to heighten the sounds of the tea bubbling in the enamel mug on the stove. After a while, Mother turned and left the room. I pondered the contents of the box, and it bothered me that I could not read Mother's expression. Was Mother angry?

Farook was standing in the passage. It was obvious that Aunty Mairoonisha had not expected to see him there. She whispered something to her son, who smiled, a full movement of his facial muscles. And, leaving his mother in my bedroom, he approached me. I became completely still as Farook neared. He embraced me, holding me closely until Aunty Mairoonisha approached us. Farook turned and welcomed his mother into our embrace. We stood, arms around each other.

I returned to the table with my mug of freshly brewed tea. I was dazed by what had just happened. What ritual had been played? It was as if our embracing was a cover-up of what had transpired before. How I wished I could find the courage to speak my mind. The deadly weight of my thoughts was becoming unbearable.

I sat close to Mother, comforted by her strength. She rose when Farook came into the room, carrying the box. His face was bright, the skin creased into happy smiles. I could see in the very lucidity of his eyes that tears had glistened there, and I wondered why.

'Na'eema, I would like to have the pleasure of extending my hand in marriage to you.' He turned to face me. 'Mum would like to...'

'You mean that you are proposing to me now?' I interrupted, shocked.

Seeing Mother beginning to frown, I quickly reached down to touch her hand. 'Is it possible to give my answer after I've read the Istighara prayer?'

It was Aunty Mairoonisha's turn. 'That's not necessary, given that you both are in love. We will just make engagement today. I will put on a chain, sorted.'

'And...like that, my only daughter is betrothed to a Cockney butcher? What does her mother have to say about that?' someone interrupted.

It was Father, emerging from the backyard. He had raised his voice, trying to achieve a loud, booming authoritative effect, as suited the scene about to play out, but what we heard was a mocking whinge, like that of a hyena.

Captivated by the display of Father staggering towards us, everybody sat quietly. He settled into a chair beside Aunty Mairoonisha, broke into easy prattle, and tried to make amends for his abrupt outburst, for he could see how enraged Mother was with his name-calling. 'It is wonderful to invite you into our home, Farook.'

That afternoon, Aunty Mairoonisha, now heavily equipped with a frown on her face, tied a gold chain around my neck. Mother rushed around mixing rose water and red liquid colouring into tall crystal glasses. Father sat in an armchair facing us, and to conclude our informal engagement, read a verse from the Quraan, his trembling hands raised upwards.

I was beginning to feel as though I was making a huge mistake. Everything was moving too quickly, and Farook's mother made me uneasy. I did not like her domineering manner. She seemed as controlling as Mother. Not wanting to spoil the celebrations I knew Farook was looking forward to, I did my best to smile and appear joyful. As they got up to leave, Aunty Mairoonisha said that she would call Mother to arrange a wedding date.

Mother nodded and seriously reminded us about the evils of delaying the nikaah. 'I don't want them to date too long. It's not nice, and people talk. Na'eema's reputation is at stake. We rather make nikaah, then they can date and whatever...'

We nodded, and Aunty Mairoonisha said, 'Banoo, surely you would want to give Na'eema a big wedding since she's your only daughter.'

'I do...but I don't want them to date and all that. Anything can happen these days.'

Farook gently held his mother, gesturing for her to remain silent, but Aunty Mairoonisha reassured him, 'It is all part of the process.'

We stood on the porch for a little while, watching the children playing cricket in the street, and their voices increased in volume as they hit the ball. A headache was coming on, and I was eager for them to leave.

Farook leaned over and whispered in my ear, 'I will call you tonight, my love.'

I greeted Aunty Mairoonisha and accepted her cold embrace. I turned and went back into the house, exhausted. Something just didn't feel right.

***

It was only later that I learned that Farook was involved in politics. I visited the library and searched through back issues of newspapers, where I found his name in at least a dozen articles.

I had felt so despondent. Life around me was in constant

turmoil, student protests in the #feesmustfall movement, students getting arrested. Then suddenly, he walked in. He had bluffed his way out of slaughtering the cows, saying that he would do the meat deliveries for the day. He sat down opposite me, and his eyes fell on the article I was reading. The editorial claimed that he was involved in the recent #feesmustfall campaign at one of Johannesburg's most popular universities.

On that morning, my mother offered him a brewed cup of masala tea. I wanted him to go. He shook his head. The questions gushed from me in full stream. I demanded to know why he had kept this life away from me.

'You know they arrested and detained her for questioning.'

'Who?' I asked.

'My friend, the student who I work with.' His voice became softer.

'What happened?'

'You know… The university security, the powers that be… They made it happen. They spurred on a riot on our peaceful march.'

Did that really happen? Was she really innocent? I didn't ask. It wasn't the time to. I merely reached for his hand and held on tightly in a supportive way when consoling a hurting friend. We sat in silence for a moment, lost in our own thoughts.

'Listen, I'm going to her house later. Would you like to come along?' he asked.

'To her home?'

'Yes, to lend support to the family…'

'Wouldn't it be odd having me there?'

'No, I will introduce you as my fiancée,' he responded shyly.

Hours later, in a meditative moment, he told me how he had come to look for me when he'd realised that he could have been arrested, and I would not have knowledge of his whereabouts. He also confessed that he had been scared that I would reject him once I knew how involved he was in fighting for free education with the students.

Shortly after, I joined him on the front stoep. I wore a long skirt, a long-sleeved blouse – as he'd suggested – and a draped black scarf favoured by the older Muslim aunties. He led me to the van which was parked behind my father's Toyota Corolla. When he opened the door, I collected my skirt and climbed into the passenger side. The beige leather bore cuts in them like markings of age, and the van wore a scent of blood, bitter and sour. Did he own another car? I didn't have the nerve to ask him.

At the home of his comrade, Farook led me through the small black gate along the path to the front door. Pairs of shoes patterned the entrance. He bent down to untie his laces and remove his shoes. I was surprised when he beckoned for me to do the same. I was happy that I had worn knee-high stockings. I did not like to walk barefoot, especially on ground foreign to me.

'Hey, we Muslims are well acquainted with removing our shoes and walking barefoot in sacred spaces...' he announced to nobody.

'Not me.' I studied my stockings for rips and tears and found a distinct ripple leading to a large hole at the sole. 'I'm okay with it if I'm aware of the expectation. Then I can prepare.' I shrugged. There was nothing I could possibly do now, given the circumstances. He smiled then continued ahead, nudged open the front door, and stepped into the house. I followed him. I was relieved he hadn't launched into consolation and good counsel about my beauty, character, and other so-called dignified traits he thought I possessed. This behaviour is common in the earlier days of romantic courtship when couples are all about wooing each other. I was never one for all that superficial banter. And so I found it quite endearing that he did not bother with the practice.

Sensing my unease, Farook slipped my hand into his and gently led me into the house. In the lounge, a large group of women dressed in black cloaks sat huddled in groups reading the Quraan. Others sat praying with tasbeehs. Mrs Ebrahim was waiting for Farook, it seemed, because she stood up, swaying uneasily on her feet. Farook moved in closer to her and gently wrapped her into a secure embrace. A small child of around four years old clung to Mrs Ebrahim's white cloak. The older woman put a protective arm over her. The sense of fear was devious; it was an unseen, illusory creature that haunted this family.

I remember the anger I had felt then, and my heart went out to little Sameera. Seeing her innocence destroyed with the knowledge that her mother had been arrested was too much for me to handle. Nelson Mandela and his comrades had been locked away for twenty-seven years. Families had survived without breadwinners. Children had grown up fatherless. Did Yusra Ebrahim seek the same future for her small daughter? What about her family? I was nauseous then. I didn't want the same for myself and my children. I was particularly concerned about Farook, my soon-to-be husband. He seemed totally committed to this struggle. Even now, in the face of the dreadful reality of the situation, he was still bewitched into thinking that he was some sort of freedom fighter, a superhero who would be able to fight the government. Fight with what? Words, protests, letters? Fuck that! In between sobs, Mrs Ebrahim explained that the university had phoned to explain that Yusra had been expelled from the institution for her criminal activity. She said that little Sameera had taken the phone from her and begged the caller to let her mummy study. Farook bent down to pick up the child then, holding her head firmly to his chest. There were no more words to be said.

On leaving the house, he reached for my hand again, a gesture of solidarity – an offering of peace. I pulled away my hand. I needed to be alone. I needed space to think. I was struggling to fully comprehend the emotional upheaval of the Ebrahim household. Little Sameera's sadness followed me.

'Please take me home,' I said. There! That was the moment I decided to break off the engagement – perhaps a reckless decision in my turmoil of emotions.

I knew that I sought to anger Farook. I had silently hoped that he would dissolve into an onslaught of obscenities about my change of behaviour towards him. Maybe his anger would release the wrath and grief that had occupied my mind. I wanted to scream and cry. I felt so vulnerable and exposed, sitting there in the van alongside him.

He gripped the steering wheel firmly, and his eyes did not leave the road. Perhaps I had wanted more; I am not so sure even now, seven years later. Perhaps I wanted him to reach for me with promises that everything would be okay for us. I needed him to assure me that the Ebrahim household would heal again and that the scars of that horrifying experience would slowly disappear for little Sameera and her Naani, with new growth and restoration. I was disappointed that he showed so much emotion to little Sameera and her grandmother, but he failed to extend the same level of sentiment to me – his soon-to-be wife. How involved was he in activism? Would I be a second wife? The many questions seemed like an onslaught to my very being.

Farook did not speak a single word. The minutes dragged on.

When the van finally stopped in front of my house, the smell of blood still lingered in the air. Farook leaned over and pushed open the door. He had earlier explained that it got stuck from inside. When I looked at him, I was surprised to see his eyes closed. I waited. When he opened them again, his gaze was withdrawn and aloof.

'Na'eema, you disappoint me...'

I sat there stunned. There was so much that I wanted to say but didn't. When I got out, he pulled the door closed, revved the engine, and drove off. That was the last time that I saw him, apart from the photographs that continued to feature in newspapers and later, pre-elections on billboards and street light poles. I now see him in the many regrets I carry with me.

That night, my parents bestowed upon me my human ability to feel deep remorse for my selfish decisions, or so they put it. I spoke to them and begged them to understand why I could not marry Farook. I tried my best to justify my actions. My mother ranted about the embarrassment she would face in the community. My father complained about the large sums of money I had wasted on the many expenses incurred.

News got around quickly. My khalas and foois called Mother to sympathise and admonish her for my decisions. They spoke of the sacrifices that political leaders had made for us, for our freedom in this country. They said that I was selfish and entitled, and they were shocked by my actions. They said that nobody would choose to marry me after this. Mother relayed all of this to Father, always in my presence – often to hambraveh me. Aunty Mairoonisha phoned to request that the chain be returned. The Lenasia Times newspaper featured our story in their panchat column. The article painted me with a red brush, making me sound inhuman and uncaring.

It was then that our neighbour, Aunty Bibi, took me to visit Aunty Zohra Asvat, the widow of the late Dr Abu Baker Asvat – also known as 'Hurley' to so many. A road leading into Lenasia has been named after him. Aunty Zohra invited us into her home and fried delicious samosas for us. She spoke about her late husband as partner, father, and activist. He had been involved in initiatives aimed at improving the health of rural black South Africans during Apartheid. He had been murdered in his surgery, leaving three young children – ages six, nine, and eleven at the time. Aunty Zohra was not a bitter woman – she was proud of the work her husband had accomplished during his term. She was happy that she had contributed, too, in her own small way to the lives of so many. She related past incidents of when Dr Asvat would call her to cook meals for the poor people who came to seek refuge in their home. Sitting with Aunty Zohra, I felt guilt and deep regret for rejecting Farook. I could have told him my fears but I hadn't. Farook and Dr Asvat were the chosen ones – they had been entrusted by Allah to help others, to make a difference. Farook was not abusing drugs, he was not a gambler or a womaniser. He was fighting a worthy cause! It was then, in the company of Mrs Asvat, that I realised how selfishly I had reacted.

After my visit, I begged Mother to call Aunty Mairoonisha to request a meeting with Farook, but he did not honour our request. The Lenasia Times published a continuation of our story. A cartoonist had drawn a picture of me running after Farook, and him, with his back to me. The article made me embarrassed and angry. I despised the negative attention the media was giving me. Mrs Hassam, the principal of the school where I worked, suggested that I hand in my resignation – she explained that the publicity was bad for the school's public image.

People chose not to invite us to weddings and functions, and it hurt my mother when she discovered that invitations would not come our way. Everywhere I went, people's eyes followed me, and I could hear their hushed whispers. Buying meat became an ordeal because all the butcheries were owned by Cockneys and some were family to the Saleys.

It was then that my parents decided that it would be best if I left Lenasia. They had applied through an agency for me to teach in Dubai. "With her gone, the panchat will soon die down...!" I overheard Mother tell Father. I cried then and begged them not to send me away. Mother's mind was made up, and there was no changing it.

It's been seven years and no suitors have called. Mother often laments that I had let a 'good' boy go. I often ignore Mother's calls and have not encouraged them to visit me. I have made friends and I am keeping busy, but I find that I still yearn for home, for my former school, and my friends. Seeing couples together makes me feel sad and depressed. I cry then and I then binge eat and cry some more.

I regret my selfish actions... I regret letting Farook go...

Lockdown

Does it really matter to you, why I did it? You have, of course, formed your own impression of me, even before the scandalous gossip ran rampant, threading through the social media like termites in wood. You have probably questioned whether I considered my children before I performed the act. You consider me a *haraami* – forbidden – don't you? You have conveniently forgotten that our past moulds the experiences of the years to come. Maybe knowing more about the circumstances will make you think differently about me, but it won't change what happened on that day twenty-eight days ago.

There were bad dreams. Whenever the children took my phone, I panicked. Sometimes, when you came home, I heard voices, before realising that they were yours in a mixture of tones when you played pranks on the kids. I was thrown into oblivion once, when at the Spur, we met your buddies, and you shook hands, bumping chests. Their eyes held secrets untold. And that was when I realised that no one looks twice at someone who acts like she has nothing to hide.

Believe what you want, but be prepared to answer this question. In my shoes, how do you know you wouldn't have done the same thing?

That moment when you found out, that moment when I saw the disappointment in your eyes, I was surprised that with all the loathing and bad feelings that had surfaced, love also spilled through. It was then that I had realised that you really did love me.

I know that you were planning to send me away, discard me like used, tattered clothing. I accepted this fate. I had other plans.

And then to our disappointment, our president made the announcement that we would be in lockdown for twenty-one days and counting. On that day, when I changed into my pyjamas, I also transformed into the woman I once was. I stared at her in the mirror. I saw what you see. My eyes had lost their glamour, thus deepening the darkness around them. My skin appeared mottled, with age lines and grey blemishes. My hair turned silver grey, even though I am only in my mid-thirties. I hung up my designer clothing and packed away my heels, opting for slipslops. I despised her, that woman in the mirror. I despised me. I yearned for that world outside, that world that beckoned to me, where I chose my own stage.

We are now trapped together in lockdown. They say that this social isolation will slow the virus's spread so that fewer people need to seek treatment at any given time. They did not consider how I would cope in isolation with you.

I sometimes wonder if this is a world conspiracy to rattle the economies of most countries worldwide. Maybe we are living *The Truman Show*? We are pawns on a chess board, but this time I have decided to take matters into my own hands.

For nineteen hours a day, I am occupied with the children. The final five hours, I will myself to sleep, often with painkillers. You have hidden the strong stuff. I have asked twice daily to speak to you; I thought that everyone is given a second chance, but the cruel reality is that only happens in books and on television. I wait for my mother, but she hasn't come, either. You keep telling me that she has passed away, but I cry in anguish over the lies you dare to speak. Perhaps I will only see her when we break out.

It never gets dark in lockdown, and it never grows quiet. The sound is a symphony: the continuous racket of cartoon characters on the television; the children singing loudly and then shouting and complaining, urging me to intervene; the whirr of the electric eggbeater preparing cakes and desserts; the fridge doors and cupboard doors being opened and closed; and the *click-click-click* of plastic on plastic as the children play side by side, hitting Lego pieces with tiny hands. And even at midnight, when I toss around in bed, I can still hear the hum from the motor of the fish tank.

The only way I can stand it is to keep busy, and I do, the intense irritation that I feel within me threatening to erupt into a volcano gushing loud, obscene profanities. I scream and shout and nag. I am always begging the children to make wudhu and read their salaah. I offer them treats. I also bargain with them daily to bathe and to brush their teeth. They don't listen, and they test my patience, which is slowly waning.

I eat chocolate, slabs at a time. I devour them before I retire to the bed that we still share. I write lists of the groceries that we need, and you go out every second day or on a Friday after you read in congregation at your friend's house the Jummah salaah. I always include chocolate as an essential item on each list. You allow me to indulge. I don't know why you do that, but sometimes it makes me feel warm inside, like you are possibly trying to understand me.

I sit on the musalah, and I pray and beg for pardon. I am trying to connect with the God that I once selfishly discarded.

I often try to decipher the problems that ensnared our marriage. They are like the molehills in our garden: we see the collection of heaps of sand, but we cannot be rid of them because the moles continue to exist in our space. There is abundance of fresh earth underneath, but the molehills prevent flowers from flourishing. This is our marriage. Our flowers refuse to grow. The roots are rotting away.

Ours was an arranged marriage. You were eligible in all aspects. 'The full package!' the aunty who brought you home had said. It was only after that I realised I was a rebound from a previous relationship gone wrong. I remember in the early years of our marriage, at family gatherings, your cousins would say things, in soft whispers and loud, bashful outbursts. You always silenced them with the glares you cast their way, like heat blazing from burning coals. I asked, and you refused to tell me. You always changed the subject.

Today, the children are fighting. They are always fighting, and their silly bickering has become a game to keep them busy, to help pass time. You have forbidden that they go out to play. The neighbourhood committee complained that they were making a racket. They do. Releasing them from the confines of this house is like unlocking the cages of wild animals. After reading the contents of the message from the committee, you asked me to create activities to keep the children busy indoors. Your tone signalled that I dare not object.

I occupied them in challenges after doing hours of school and madressah work. The teachers send too many activities for me to do with them. The Apas require that I teach them Quran and Surahs and Duahs and Hadeeth and Fiqh and Aqaaid and Islamic history. The lessons are endless, spanning time and space. I teach, and they learn. I repeat, and they repeat. Then I video them to send to the madressah staff. It's all a crazy rat race with the Zoom lessons and videos being sent on Google Teams and WhatsApp. Our youngest has diarrhoea, and I have changed his napkin far too often to count, patting his reddened skin with a herbal ointment. He cries, and you say that he is ill. You say it like it is my fault. My head throbs now. I have dumped them in front of the television screen. They are arguing. They cannot compromise on a series to watch. They find bottles in a box. There are broken pieces of glass in there, too. The shards fall to the floor and our middle son gets cut. Red blood seeps through. He tries to act brave, but the tears well up and then spill out.

I did, too, you know. I tried to be brave. Once.

Problem was that there was nobody to wipe away my tears.

I have swallowed a few painkillers and heated a bean bag in the microwave. I rub my aching head using Vicks. I lie here, oblivious to the sounds that decorate my world. I am numb. I zone out, imagining your first meeting with her.

***

She was parading as a waitress in an upmarket restaurant in Sandton City frequented by the upper class. You wandered in, dazed, after having worked all day. You saw one of the patrons chatting her up, and you hurled yourself at him.

As it turned out, they were shooting an advert for a brand of tea. You didn't know that. You launched into a little speech about her being your younger sister and how you were there to protect her. Ooh, how she despised you in that moment. It wasn't your rough, ranger-guy appearance, or your audacity to act all bravado that sent her head spinning; it was the fact that you believed that she needed your help.

She was one of the affluent Houghton Muslims who screenshot their lives on Instagram in front of everyone's lives – as influencer, YouTuber, and celebrity. The only reason she was even in that restaurant on that day was because of the advert. The yeasty smell of the garlic, leaking from the kitchen behind the sit-down area of the restaurant, made her think of her mother's kitchen, a place where she never ventured. She chose to ignore the odour that was gnawing at her insides because she believed this advert would earn her more fans. Every time she received one more 'like' or 'share', she grew a larger head. She was confident that, at this rate, sooner or later, she would be the winner of the Nickelodeon Kids' Choice Awards. She had already surpassed the popularity of Lasizwe, Naqiyah Mayet, and Siddiqa Soofie put together.

She slapped you hard across the face, she was so angry. You were oblivious to the cameras or the camera crew. You grabbed her and roughly planted a kiss on her very surprised open mouth.

'Don't you dare!' she screamed, pushing you off her.

You started to laugh. 'Aneesa Patel, doll! You will be my wife soon!'

She looked at you, and a wave of surprise glinted in her eyes. Why the act when you already knew who she was? She wondered for only a moment, but she wanted you to know that a relationship was not on the cards. She was possessed of an urgency to make you understand who she was: a woman who did not live in the same world as you. So she tossed her handbag over her shoulder and stalked out.

***

That's the way I dream it happened, and I often wonder about that kiss. Did your tongue caress hers?

Social media devoured the incident, and Aneesa's accounts were ablaze. Her phone rang off the hook with requests for social appearances. They branded you "Handsome Stranger" and you wore the nickname with pride. You dressed the way you thought she'd like you to. You tagged her everywhere you went, and on all platforms, and you copied all the expressions and quotes she used. You stalked her. You were always in her presence. You were her poodle.

But she didn't see you or bother with your true identity.

How did your love story end? I don't remember...

I think I must have dozed off then.

It is dark outside when I awake. The curtains are open. They cover the small box window situated a metre beneath the ceiling. The walls are sterile white. The smells of cleaning chemicals assault my senses. The light from the corridor shifts and then drifts in. Trolley wheels slide on the polished floors; a machine beeps in tune. I am angry and frustrated suddenly. Where am I? Why is the window so high? How will I peep out to watch the children below, playing in the garden?

And then I remember that they are not allowed out. I think that they are probably sleeping. Now I can finally rest. What is the time? I scan the walls, looking for the digital clock that hangs above the door. It is not there.

When the discussion took place that afternoon at lunchtime, I wandered around the kitchen, not really fitting anywhere. You had forbidden me from cooking. I can't remember why. The television was turned on BBC News, the one channel we watch 24/7 in lockdown, and a reporter was discussing the world statistics of Covid-19.

"The UN report warns that three million people could die from coronavirus in Africa," the woman said.

You announced to our eldest, who is tracking the pandemic, that Covid-19 had already claimed forty-eight lives, and we were on day 20 of lockdown. I wondered how many more people would take their lives because of depression in lockdown. You exclaimed that President Cyril Ramaphosa is likely to extend lockdown.

'How many more days?' I asked, but you did not hear me.

You continued to stare at your cellphone screen while swiping through the tabloids.

I reach for my phone, but it is not where I left it. It is not in the kitchen attached to the charger. I find it lying on the dressing table, a replica phone toy for our three-year-old. He punches the digits, and they light up in a rainbow of colours singing classical music tunes. He cries out when I make a grab for it, and the device crashes to the floor, spraying splinters of plastic with rough, uneven edges. The music is released in loud, haphazard notes, and then it all stops.

Quiet.

The noise reminds me of the helium balloon, singing "Congratulations!" that you brought to the hospital when our little princess rose out of my wounded pelvis into a new life.

You'd place her on your chest and sing, 'Annie, will you love me, baby Annie?' You'd bring me little gifts from the pharmacy: whole nut chocolate slabs, roses, and that noisy balloon.

She was only three months old, our little Annie, perfect in every way, from the five toes on each of her feet to the fingers that had already learnt to grasp. She went to sleep in her cot and never woke. The doctors used words like sudden infant death syndrome or SIDS but all I heard was that our baby girl, your little Aneesa, was DEAD. I knew, even if no one was willing to say it to me, that this had been my fault. I killed our baby, the only living thing that bound our love. You knew this, too. You couldn't stand to look at me. You spent more and more time at the office.

After our baby girl's death, we went to the masjid to visit Maulana Ebrahim, who lives in a two-bedroom house behind the masjid. His waiting room was packed with others who needed cures for their many ailments: a woman who lost her job to a colleague less qualified; a father who had become ill suddenly; and a young boy who had lost his faith. We waited silently, sitting side by side on a wooden bench, watching the children run after a flattened ball which kept falling on its belly after being kicked. When it was my turn, you followed me into the maulana's study. You explained to him what had happened to our princess.

You had forgotten to ask him to heal our broken marriage.

Maulana Ibrahim dipped the sharpened nib of a feather into saffron water and wrote out verses onto a sheet of paper.

'Make Taawiz and pin to clothing," he instructed. You paid him, and then when we got home, you folded the paper into a tiny rectangle and wound Sellotape around it. You told me to carry it in my bra. That tiny plastic parcel remained safe, close to my heart, replacing your love. It delivered me somehow from a space of extreme pain into one of peace. I learnt to laugh again. Just a little, only when you were not around to see me.

Some days are sunbeams and roses and others deathly storms. There are highs and lows. The clouds gather as the wind pushes them aggressively into a storm cloud; the rain cloud that threatens to dissolve me, day in and day out. Nobody can overcome grief without love, without there being a reason to live.

You gave me a reason to die.

I think there is a part of me that knows that if I leave, if I take the children and moved away from you, you could live again. Find another Aneesa Patel, perhaps. Find another Annie.

Forbidden

When they came, I was out in the backyard, kicking a ball up the side of the house, with anger that choked me so much I could hardly control my kick. I had struggled through the torrential rain, blinking away the water that shaded my vision, and I continued like a soldier in battle. I kicked the ball with force, watched as it smashed into the wall, and then leapt back like a frog into wet mud. Rain fell, sliding over the dirty stain the wall wore. I kicked the ball again and again – marking the wall – tattooing it with a brown ugly stain like the one found on the side of my face.

'Sideburns,' they mocked me. It had become my nickname. Children in their virgin innocence are cruel. It had hurt me at first, but Mother explained that I had been born with the birthmark, and if I ignored the name-callers, they were likely to find somebody else to pick on. I couldn't ignore them. I always lashed out to protect myself, and when I did that, they often called me other names like *Coloured*, *Bushy*, and even *Bastard*. They said that I didn't look like my parents – I looked *different*. The term *different*, the way they said it with a twang, always held a negative connotation, like it symbolised something criminal. I fought back, and as Mother had predicted, I became stronger. My nickname *Sideburns* stuck with me like the dried piece of gum wedged into the grooves of a school shoe – stubborn, hard, and dirty. I eventually accepted that the nickname had found me, and I wore it with gangster pride. Somehow, now at fifteen, it defined me.

'Uzair! Stop punching that ball! The racket has given me a headache.'

It was Mother, trudging through the rain towards me. I held

the ball still, balancing it with the toe of my shoe. It rolled away, and its wet skin threatened to slip into the mud. I held on.

'Are they still here?'

'Yes, they are.'

'What do they want this time?' I asked.

She gnawed at the loose skin on the edge of her thumb and shrugged. Mother began to say something but stopped and looked down at her thumb as if she had remembered something. The rainwater hung in her hair like connected threads of silk.

'What do they want, Mother? Tell me,' I begged.

She lifted her head and searched my face but avoided looking into my eyes. The heat in her gaze alarmed me, making me feel older than she was.

'Please, Uzair, not now! You know that Daadi is not well! I have too much on my mind.' Mother kicked away the ball. 'Let's go in.'

'Tell me, please, Mother. Tell me.' She had no right to avoid telling me; I knew why I pleaded, I needed to know what was going on.

I approached her, so angry I felt out of control. The rain pelted down, drenching the grass and sand, while the sky lay hidden beneath a dense blanket of cloud. I thought of the angry sky – so dark and foreboding. I wanted suddenly very much to disappear. I longed for a puff from my hookah pipe. I felt the smoke uncoiling from my nostrils into a serpent dance. It would make me feel happy. I craved that feeling.

'Uzair—' She made it sound like a bad word.

I turned away. 'Leave me!' I wanted to be alone. I wanted to have time to understand what was happening. If she didn't want to tell me, I needed the space to try to fathom it out for myself.

Silence.

'I'm sorry.'

Meaningless words.

I reached for the ball, dribbled it, then kicked. I felt her eyes on me. The ball ricocheted off the wall and banged into the side of my head. I swayed, unbalanced, grasping my head. Nausea churned inside me, as strong as the piercing pain in my head. I rocked my body from side to side and tried to dissolve away the dizziness. I closed my eyes and breathed in the smells of wet mud, the blossoming scent of young guavas, and the far-off stench of a dead rat. I could still feel her looking at me. Her gaze raised hairs along my spine. I cursed.

'Uzair, no...' she pleaded.

I turned to look at her.

She was crying. In that moment, I forgot my anger. Her sorrow hung on her like a haggard garment sewn for an old woman. I wanted to reach out to hold her the way I had as a child, but something held me back. In her eyes lay black pools of pity.

Abruptly, she turned away, and I was left staring after her, pondering her disappointment in me.

With her leaving, a new kind of anger gnawed at me. I was going to have to wait for the revelation – until she was ready to tell or better yet, until somebody babbled. I couldn't wait a second longer. The uncertainty was consuming me.

The door banged shut. I let out a deep sigh. I felt defeated. At my feet, a blanket of green lawn led across a large backyard to a small patio framed with a cage of black steel panels. The house was double-storeyed, built of grey-painted walls, with rectangular burglar-barred windows revealing life beyond. Black tiles had been laid along the top, which formed a triangular roof. The chimney straddled the middle like a centrepiece. A house this big held four entrances – built ideally for the two families who had once occupied it.

Before I had time to think, I crossed the yard and passed through the caged patio to the glass-panelled back door. The door stood ajar. I paused and listened. A few shards of words escaped through the opening.

'How dare you take that! You don't have the right to...who gives you the right to?'

The light beyond the door rocked to and fro, and as I waited, I saw the haphazard movement of my mother's hands. I pushed open the door.

My mother was standing at the fireplace with a scorching red face. My late father's brother, whom I call Iqbal Papa, stood in the archway near the front door. Between them, on the thick, chocolate-brown carpet, was a tribe of large, taped boxes. My mother looked suddenly from my uncle to me and moved to the boxes. A slow billow of fire danced against the glass of the anthracite stove.

'What's going on here?' I asked.

My uncle gave me a doubtful, aggressive stare, as if he belonged here, and I didn't. 'Shut up, boy! Sit!'

Those're our belongings, I wanted to say... but when I saw Iqbal Papa's expression, I struggled to get the words free.

'No!' Mother reached for the boxes again but then pulled away, as if they had scalded her.

'Get out of here, Ruwaida! Go! These belong to me now!'

'It's ours...' Mother sank slowly back on to her seat on the pouffe next to the stove.

No, I wanted to say, *no, don't speak to us like that, this is our house!* But something held me still. It bothered me that Mother had succumbed to the corner, accepting defeat. I moved forward, purposely, and reached for a box, delving through its contents. I took in the transparent plastic parts of Mother's food processor, the razor-edged blade, twined wires and plugs, recipe books... But there was too much in there, and my mind triggered alarms I couldn't comprehend.

Iqbal Papa sauntered hastily to the boxes. I should have pulled them away and guarded them, but my uncle quickly hauled each box into the waiting hands of his helper, Oom Hans. He performed this task with such assurance, it was done before I could say anything. He opened one or two boxes and rummaged through their contents before closing them with eager resolution. He paused once, smirking at the contents of one of the boxes, which he then closed and handled with more care than the others.

The front door opened, and someone asked, 'Where's the boy? *Sideburns?*'

I started towards the door, but Mother motioned that I remain in my place. Riyaad Papa appeared in the archway and gestured a greeting with his hand.

'Salaam.' He went straight past his brother and took my mother's hands in both of his. His long white kurta hung wet at his feet and had brown marks at the hem. He was old, and the bushy white beard he wore on his bony face gave him a kind of harshness. Now I could see why Riyaad Papa stood as head of Munshi tribe. He was ruthless.

'Ruwaida, forgive me,' he said. 'Your boy is old enough to join the business now. It's time for him to seek penance for his father's debt.'

'No!' screamed Mother. 'Uzair is just a child. He needs to complete school. I will not allow him to join the business... Not now or ever!'

Something like sadness glinted in the older man's eyes, but when Riyaad Papa turned to look at me, his face was perfectly composed. 'You will join us, boy. Your mother knows that the debt needs to be paid.'

Mother stared ahead, and the veins on her forehead grew thick and dark as if something would explode from within. 'I promised to pay back every cent...'

There was silence. The purr of the rain splattered against the window-glass. The room was glum and dark, and it made Mother's face pale and ghastly.

Iqbal Papa set a teapot and two mugs of hot tea down carefully on the television cabinet. A thin cord of steam grew from it and disappeared into the air. The knock of the glass on the wood was as loud as the blows of a hammer on a nail.

'What if I refuse to go?'

'You don't have a choice, eh! But come now, you are tough, right! They don't call you *Sideburns* for nothing.' Riyaad Papa sniggered.

'Oh, my love,' Mother said. 'This has nothing to do with you.' Her eyes went to Riyaad Papa. 'The debt was your father's and now mine to pay...'

'Ag, come now, Ruwaida. You know that you don't have the money. The boy is of age to join us – working in the business is as honest a trade as can be. And he will learn way more there than in any school. You can't deny that, dearest!'

My heart drummed fiercely in its cage.

A stifling silence stretched out while Iqbal Papa enjoyed his tea with loud slurps.

'Maybe it's not what I would have wanted to do with my life.' I sucked in air deeply. 'I will go – it seems to be the right thing to do—'

Mother pressed her fingers into the vein on her forehead, rubbing it to loosen the tension.

'No, you will not! This is not what Hoosein would have wanted for our son!'

Riyaad Papa plodded across to the television cabinet, bent down, and poured masala tea from the teapot into a mug. The scent of the strong spices assaulted the air.

'What! Hoosein didn't care a shit about either of you!' He downed the tea in one long gulp. He pulled out a cotton handkerchief from his kurta pocket and sneezed into it.

'Ruwaida, maybe you should be grateful. We are letting you off easy. At least...you still have a roof over your heads.'

The vein on Mother's forehead throbbed. 'I only want...'

Riyaad Papa wiped his handkerchief across his lips, then viciously hurled the mug at the flatscreen television screen. It shattered, puncturing a web of lines into the glass. Mother made a choking sound and buried her face in the bowls of her hands.

Riyaad Papa turned to face us and laughed. 'Watching television is a forbidden act in Islam. Owning one is an act of blasphemy...'

Iqbal Papa cleared his throat.

'I will work for you,' I said.

Mother had lifted her legs and curled them under her. She hugged herself, her head resting on the arm of the sofa.

'Mother? It's going to be okay—" I pulled her gently to sit upright, dismayed at how old she seemed. Her face was whitish; the cold had seeped into her bones. She shivered, and I bent down close to her to hold her.

'It's going to be all right,' I said.

She stared past me, into the burning coals of the fire.

She kept shaking her head, her lips tightly pursed. I looked up and stared at my two older uncles. They showed no sign of leaving. I couldn't understand why Mother put up with them, but without her permission, I couldn't tell them to go.

I stood up. I needed to get out of the house.

She caught at my hand. 'Uzair.' Her eyes glazed over. 'I'm so sorry.'

I couldn't look at her. I struggled to the door. Outside, the sun tried earnestly to squeeze out between two bands of clouds. I looked down at the colours that played in the collected water puddles. I blinked. And then...the sun had gone, and the dark clouds patterned the sky once more. A hadada ibis screamed in a nearby tree.

I returned to the section of the garden where I had been kicking earlier. The drenched ball now lay cushioned on a clump of mud. I sagged against the wall. Riyaad Papa's voice rang in my ears. *Hoosein didn't care a shit about either of you.*

He was wrong. My father loved us. We were his life. Despair grew inside me, an illness attacking my vital organs. I couldn't remember a time like this. My memories, my past was happy. We had always been happy. Last spring, last winter, were coloured with momentous celebrations, as if contentment and happiness would always be ours. I closed my eyes. I could still see the three of us, bound closely by love, them binding me in their visible affection for each other.

Something whispered behind me, demanding entry to the beauty of my memories, eradicating all the happiness with rot and decay. It was real, and it masked the rain and the screeching hadadas. I blocked my ears and tried to shut it out.

'Uzair!' Mother cried. 'Daadi has taken a turn for the worse! Quick, hurry!'

I waited. Bitterness and confusion hauled me into a turmoil of uncertainty. With my Daadi ill, this was no one's house but mine. I could sell the house, pay the debt, and then Mother and I could move to a small flat close to a university. I stood for a long time with one foot raised behind me on the wall behind. I needed to think things through. I felt happier knowing there was still hope for us. At last, I went into the house. The lounge lay empty. I followed their voices upstairs. Thick lumps of wet mud from the soles of their shoes were strewn on the carpeted staircase.

I knocked. 'Salaam,' I announced.

It was Riyaad Papa who said, 'We are busy Uzair, come back later.'

I stood on the other side of the closed door. The outside grey spilt through the bathroom window, masking everything in shadows. I could hear them talking in undertones. I edged closer, with my ear to the door. Their voices were barely audible.

'...we...signature...' Iqbal Papa said. 'Mother, Ma, can you hear me?' he called louder.

'Iqbal, Riyaad!' Mother cried. 'You are frustrating our mother. She is in no condition for this!'

'And that will suit you just fine, won't it Ruwaida?' Riyaad Papa grunted. 'I know that Mother dearest can hear us and will sign the damn papers, even if we make her do it!'

'Shame on you! Sies! You were always a dog, Riyaad!'

'Please, Ruwaida,' says Iqbal Papa. 'You know that we won't do that. Shame, you have been through too much today.' He coughed and tried to clear his throat, and it sounded like he was choking on blobs of phlegm. 'I really think that it's best that you nap for a little while. It's going to be a long night.'

I didn't wait for Mother. I couldn't deal with all the unspoken emotions we now shared. Not yet, anyway. I went into the passage with a sense of uneasiness. I hadn't had anything to eat since the morning, and now, as evening set in, the emotions of the day had gnawed a pit of hunger deep into my stomach. I was starving. I found myself downstairs in the kitchen, wolfing down slices of white bread lathered with mango atchaar. With determined resolution to silence my thoughts, I set myself a few chores. I stoked the anthracite stove noisily because the house was too quiet – I needed to break the silence. I washed the dishes, and I completed tasks that I would ordinarily watch Mother do. When I collapsed, an hour later, with my forehead on the prayer mat, I was so exhausted I fell asleep with my head between my outstretched palms.

I woke out of a dream of a raging blizzard. My face lay hidden in my hands, to protect myself from the stinging icy wind. I'd been running away from angry barking wolves that looked like a broad silhouette in the deathly storm. I was out of air, and for a minute, the cold bit into my throat. But that sensation quickly dissipated when I finally realised where I was. The room was dark; the fire had died. I tried to sit up. My body hurt all over with cold. A tremor took hold of me, and I hugged myself tightly. Tension blinded my vision and pricked along my temples.

Shouting.

That was what had woken me: crying and angry rants like heated sirens signalling danger. I dragged myself to the passage.

Riyaad Papa's voice, breathless. 'Get out of this house! Take your boy with you! You don't belong here anymore!'

I clenched my teeth, grinding down on the molars. I climbed the stairs, holding onto the wall for support. It was too dark. Something lay there in the darkness. I turned around. Nothing. I took another step and bumped into it. Mother was sitting on the top step. Her eyes were open, staring at me. Her face shone moonlit pale in the darkness.

'Mother, Mother, what's happening? Is Daadi okay?'

'Daadi is gone,' she muttered. 'We have to leave, too.'

'I don't understand. This is our house.' I dropped to my haunches on the lower step in front of her, so that I could look up into her face. I wrapped her two hands in mine. 'Mother, look at me! We are not leaving. This house belongs to us now! Daadi would have wanted that!'

She pushed me, and I fell backwards, off balance.

'Fuck!'

Mother shuddered. 'No, Uzair. No, my child.' We stared at each other through the thick darkness. 'I'm so sorry.'

There was a screech of chair legs on tiles from downstairs. Riyaad Papa sang. 'Sideburns, oh Sideburns, can you come sort out some candles here? I can't see a fucking thing!'

Mother shifted her weight on the step. Her face was gleaming with wet tears.

'It's all right, Ma, I will go. You stay here.'

I didn't know how I reached the kitchen or lit the candles in their trays, but the house seemed alive once more.

Iqbal Papa suddenly appeared in front of me. Behind him Riyaad Papa waited.

'Where's your mother?' Iqbal Papa barked.

'What do you want from us?'

'My dearest mother has passed away, boy, and you have the audacity to question me!' Iqbal Papa spat.

I swallowed.

'*Sideburns* the troublemaker.' Riyaad Papa sniggered. 'He was never really one of us, eh, Brother?'

Mother's voice cut in, from behind me. 'No! Leave my son!'

For a second, I thought they were going to say something. They shared a quick look.

Iqbal Papa grunted. 'The funeral is tonight at ten.'

He pushed ahead of us and went to the telephone in the hallway. 'Move the furniture. The burial committee will bring blankets. Oh, and make a new fire. This house is freezing cold!' To Mother he said, 'Ruwaida, you can assist them with the body preparation. They can use the kitchen.'

I clenched my jaw without answering. I wanted to tell him to move the furniture by himself – or something fouler – but the thought of Mother's vulnerability and my Daadi lying cold upstairs made me swallow the words. And anyway, I only had a short time to put up with them before they left us for good.

I collected the coal and the firewood from outside. I forced myself to clean the grate and make a new fire. I lit the fuel and waited until the flames had taken hold. I then went up to Daadi's room. There was such a busy banter in there that it felt like walking into a gathering of whispered secrets. Everything, apart from the window, was bright and airy. Beyond the windowpane, the first bands of night shifted the light of the day, giving the horizon a black-orange tint. The members of the burial committee scurried across the room – clearing away the clutter – to enable a pathway for the hospital bed with Daadi in it to be carried out.

I stood at the side of the bed and lifted her hand in mine. I expected her to turn to me then. I longed to see her laughing eyes, but she just lay there, her smile lost in the gaunt, shrunken non-human who had stolen her. I felt cheated, and it angered me. They had stolen my last moments with her. I reeled across to the corner of the room and leant against the window. It was hard to breath.

'Shut up!' I shouted. 'My Daadi is sleeping!'

Silence.

The windows rattled in their metallic cages. The rain continued to pour. The air was hot with a strong reek of camphor.

I clambered to her and climbed onto the bed. I buried my head in Daadi's bosom, the way I had as a child.

'What in God's name are you doing, Uzair?'

The words broke the spell. I jumped instinctively, blinking through my tears. It was Mother – and the others behind her – Riyaad Papa, Iqbal Papa.

'Uzair, I asked what do you think you were doing!' But she didn't wait for an answer before she hastily pulled me off the bed. *I'm greeting my grandmother*, I wanted to say, *just a final goodbye...*

But when I saw the anger in Mother's eyes, I swallowed the words.

'Haraami!' screamed Iqbal Papa.

'No, don't say that!' Mother held me and dragged me with her to the door.

She looked me squarely in the eyes. 'We, you...need to leave now. Do you understand?'

I didn't. What had happened? I was saying goodbye to Daadi, but somehow, I had done something unforgivable. I shook my head.

'You have to leave now, Uzair,' Mother pleaded. 'You are not wanted here! Naani is here to take you to Laudium. I will join you later, after the three days of mourning.'

'Now?' I turned to her so fast that my hair stung the side of her face.

'For Allah's sake, Uzair!' Mother ground her fingers tighter into mine. 'Don't make this any harder. You think I want us to leave? This is our home...was our home... Do you think that after I tried so hard to bring you up with love...'

'Ruwaida, I think that it's time you told the boy the truth,' Iqbal Papa said softly.

'Nooo...' whined Mother, defeated.

'It is necessary! Besides, the boy should have been told years ago... It is his right to know!'

They had moved away out of the room, beyond the snooping ears of the burial committee ladies. I looked at Mother. She avoided my gaze, her shoulders hunched over, and her hand holding her chest in defeat.

'Boy, Uzair... You are not from us. You are forbidden to your grandmother. You cannot hold her,' Iqbal Papa said. 'Uzair, you were adopted at birth. You are no longer allowed here. This house is now ours. It's best that you leave now...to avoid further embarrassment to us! We are sorry.'

I turned. I didn't want to hear any more. I was adopted... It suddenly made sense, and then, it didn't. I tried to block it all out, but their voices followed me... Their voices haunted me like the echoes in the wind.

The Tears of the Weaver

I remember. On the soft sofa in our living room, large cushions and smaller ones wedged between us to separate us, to show us the zones we were meant to own. The screen flittering with pictures and sounds, dead to my ears; you captivated and excited – you beckoning the film to bring death – me terrified with fear, trying to block it all out.

It isn't just that I remember. I feel it – that same anxiety this morning, curled up in foetal form like a baby, sobbing softly and sorrowfully, squeezing my insides to control the fear banging inside me, like the wild beats that tame a drum. I have that thing, that feeling I get when I need to piss and cannot reach the toilet in time. And I think, *I'm going to let go, I'm going to do it,* not because I want to, but because I have to. As though at that moment I would be released from the shackles of that necessity that engulfs me.

I often wonder if you remember...

What puzzles me is how well I remember. Too well. Why is it that I can remember the things that happened to me when I was only seven years old, and trying to remember what I ate last night for supper is an ordeal? The things I want to remember I can't, and the things I try so hard to forget keep awakening my insides, clawing out my very being. The harder I try to push the tears back into my eyes, the more overwhelming it becomes, that raw, undeniable pain coursing through my veins like a speed train en route to its final destination.

All that white, that staring bright light, the sterility of the bathroom, it flashes into my thoughts and brings with it a flood of memories: Dad peering through the lens of the camera to capture my awkward form of thick-framed spectacles and pigtails; you towering bashfully over me, one hand combed through your thick brown hair. Do you remember that it was my first day of primary school and you had promised Mum that you would keep an eye out for me? But you laughed with them when they pulled my pigtails, loosening the pink ribbons that bound them. You held me after, you didn't have to, but you did, and I liked it. I remember the long drives to faraway places, Father urging us to discover new sights.

'What is that?' he would ask.

I couldn't remember then. I couldn't remember that a power station released dark foreboding smoke into the sky like a serpent that swallows its prey. I confused it with a silo. Silly it was, I see that now. You always whispered the answer to every difficult question to me in exchange for the treats Mother would gift us.

Later, when we were older, you with your tattooed skin which you hid from Mother but showed off to the girls who ooh-ed and aah-ed. You pocketing Father's car keys and taking the car for a spin. It always reeked of cigarette smoke after, and I often wonder why our parents chose to ignore the stench. Why did they do that? Did they know that your innocence was lost? I remember a netball tournament. Loud chants, dancing cheerleaders with red pom-poms, all eyes on me. Hot in the face, I had missed the shot, and moans from the crowd were muted in my ears. I can still see it all, though. You, with your outstretched arms and thumbs pointed down, a sly smile creasing your eyes.

I am so deep in thought that I forget I am still lying on the bathroom floor. I am there, on the netball court; it comes to me unexpectedly, as though I have been mysteriously transported to that moment, and before I know it, I must get rid of the sourness that has risen within me. It spews out of me, green with bile and treacherous with rage.

Fully clothed, I step into the shower and turn on the water. I look up. The water pelts down onto me. My whole body is drenched. I remember this: a hot walk home from school, beckoning water from steamy mirages in the distance, you walking ahead and ignoring my calls. And then you turned and waited. The gate to Mrs Moodley's backyard stood ajar. You beckoned me to join you to take a *quick dip* in the pool. I refused. I told you that we could get caught, and you became angry and then offered a cold, merciless laugh. I can still hear your words in my head: *Ameera, grow up, will you! You are one big fat whining cry baby.* I followed you then. Into the icy cold, algae-mutated water. And after, you reached for my hand and pulled me out of the water. I can still feel what I did that day, wet clothing clinging to the warmth within my heart. I had made you happy.

I turn off the water, pull the towel off the rail, and wrap it around me. I head to the cupboard, where I open the doors and rummage for the pants I wore today. I pull out black sweatpants – the first ones I spot. No, not those – a long cut scars the material of the right leg. I open a drawer and toss the pants back in – I can't throw them away, not yet anyway – they wear their own tale. There it is, that old grey, faded mass of material – my school uniform. A tingling in the pit of my stomach, dizzy with excitement, stars dancing before my eyes; I channel myself to the bed and sit down.

The shrill cry of the phone startles me out of my daze. I reach for it, not recognising the number. I answer.

'Hello,' I say.

'Ameera, Ameera Carim?' It's the voice of an older woman, rough around the edges.

'Yes... Who is this?'

'Ameera, it's me, Aunty Hajoo. Can you please come collect your stuff? I have a tenant moving in next Friday.'

'Yes, right of course. I will,' I lie.

'Thank you,' she croaks. 'How are—'

I cut the call. I am not in the mood for small talk.

I open my bedroom door, step out, and turn towards the passage which leads to your old room. I can see you there still, lying in bed, a game console in your grasp, your eyes following the muscular warriors on the screen. Frowning, always angry.

I am awakened, stepping into your room, where I heard the sounds of slashing knives from the games you always played, and I smelled dagga – the dagga hidden in holes within the wall beside the bed. The bittersweet smell of a burning joint, and the stench spirits me back to that day.

I can't face it, those memories. I rush from the room. I pull the door closed, and it bangs shut. I half expect to hear you throw curses in my direction. The hairs on my skin rise, alert, and my head is dizzy again. I lean against the wall to regain my composure.

A tapestry in a tall, rectangular frame remains on the wall space between our rooms, its glass casing cracked. Mother wove the tapestry with her two gentle hands. The pink-and-white flowers, linked with greenish-brown leaves, are twined into an upward vine. I remember the way the glass covering reflected the light in the dimly lit passage, and how to passers-by, the vine appeared to be swaying. Remarkable talent, everyone exclaimed, and Father beamed proudly. He was always so keen to show off Mother's numerous talents. They were like shining amulets on his uniform. He had married well, they had all said.

But, like all handwoven tapestries, this one, too, holds the tears of its weaver. It holds Mother's tears. And it has been strategically placed to hide the scarred wall that displays signs of a battle once fought. That tapestry is almost perfect, while our lives wear the rot of a waning reality.

A clock is chiming, as if it comes from outside. I follow the sound through the passage, past an empty space – there used to be a dining room there, with a large wooden kiaat dining-room suite. I am not sure what has become of it.

I step into what used to the living room and stand there, looking. The room smells soiled, like the decay of a rat. For how long has it contained this smell? I can't remember when last I entered this space. It is still the same, except for the stink. Solid kiaat furniture, many books, empty shelves – the ornaments from our overseas travels have been removed, and there are no family pictures on the walls. This room does not belong to us; its identity has been washed clean. The walls all painted white, to mask the secrets untold. And then I see it. In the haziness of fatigue, the tasteless delight of terror, I see the dry blood-like stain from the chocolate ice cream that we had that night.

I remember. All those winters. Warmth from the orange-flamed fireplace. Mother, Father, you, and me sitting on that sofa, full cushions behind us, balancing platters of TV dinners on our laps. Watching SABC news.

I can't look at it; it makes me anxious and terrified, seeing that this room has accepted death. Remembering that day when we all died.

We broke off contact from you, after. We left. Mother thought it was the best way for me to deal with everything that happened. All we wanted was to be left alone, to forget Lenasia, to forget you. We needed to heal. We built a small life with a distant relative in Cape Town.

After Mother's passing, I sought you. I wrote long letters. I often reminisced about memories of family trips and experiences. I tried to analyse when and how it all went terribly wrong.

I remember: a carnival, bright lights, lazy rides, and very fast ones. A giant stuffed soft pink bear, swinging between Father and me. Happy laughter which popped like a fly-away balloon, high in the sky. You put up a tantrum because you wanted a pink bear, too. Mother felt your wrath in the punches you threw with your tight fists. You only stopped when you saw her wet face and finally registered her cries of anguish. You destroyed that bear because you couldn't have it. Later, the bear sat limp, its insides hidden under your bed. You told me never to talk about it, you made me promise, *for Mum's sake,* and so I put it away. I suppose I believed that you would be happy with me for protecting you, but you never showed happiness, and you never said sorry. And you never explained to me how it was that you could have treated me, your little sister, the way you did.

I move to the edge of the sofa, where I pull out the stained cushion seat to find gums, a half-eaten chocolate biscuit – stuffed there by a child, perhaps – coins, and cigarettes butts. Were there children at the funeral? I can't remember. I am suddenly uncomfortable, my underarms feel damp, my clothing too tight on me, so I get up from the sofa and return to the bookshelf, where I study the titles. Books everywhere. Of course. We were once collectors of fiction and non-fiction. One book stops me in my tracks. It is from the Childcraft collection, the cover a dull orange colour, small pictures stuck into rectangular borders.

'How things are made,' is the title printed on the spine. I remember: Mother selecting show-and-tells for me to do from there, you always jeering when I practised. Me complaining to Mother. Mother admonishing you to behave. You always agreed in exchange for an ice cream treat. Soft, sweet, and dark chocolate-flavoured ice cream on a sugared cone.

I remember: on that day, sitting on the sofa, discarded TV dinners. SABC news segueing into advert breaks. You wanted chocolate-flavoured ice cream. Was it a special occasion? Sweet licks of ice cream. And then you made a grab for my cone. It fell – a brown sticky mass on the sofa. I remember: ice cream in the pit of my stomach, rushing upwards. Gurgling, gasping, coughing –ice cream stuck in the wrong pipe. I could feel it pushing against the walls of my throat, seeping out of my mouth, as I spluttered.

Mother sent you away then, sent to your room. You took the car keys and left. You did not return. Father comforted Mother. *He will be all right. It's just a phase. Leave him.*

I made an excuse to do homework. I drew a card for you, a letter saying that I was sorry. I drew large hearts and painted them in red. I left my room and turned to yours. A disordered chaos of clothes and games, a teal-coloured blanket lying on the floor, a haze of sour smoke in the air, the windows left open, the curtains billowing inwards. Without thinking, I began to tidy up. I pushed the bed away from the wall. I was on your bed reaching over, retrieving dirty laundry from underneath, when I discovered the holes in the wall. I collected the stuff; I didn't know what it was then, but I knew it was something not good because you had hidden it. I took it away to my own room, stashed it in my own hiding place – with my Barbie doll and chocolates.

I went to bed but didn't sleep. I pulled up the bedcovers and lay there waiting. You had not returned, and I had no idea where you had gone.

I fell asleep.

Father woke me. He and Mother were going out to look for you. I must stay awake, he said. I was to call them as soon as you returned.

I fell asleep again; I couldn't keep my eyes open.

I woke with a shock.

You had returned. I knew, because I could hear your music, loud and angry. After a while, the music stopped, and then I could hear voices, low and then louder. *Where the fuck is it?* Your voice? I wasn't sure. I got out of bed and went out into the passage. The lights were out. I didn't know why. Your room door was open. The light from the moon drifted in. There were others with you. I couldn't make out the shadows. I could make out Mother's cries coming towards us. I didn't say anything. I was too afraid to breathe. I crouched low, on all fours. I crawled back into my bedroom, into the cupboard, and stayed there.

I remember: sitting, on plastic boxes of shoes, in between long pinafore uniforms, forgotten like a doll in a toy chest. I heard everything. Barely moving a muscle. I wrapped myself in a pinafore, muting my fearful cries. Warm liquid ran down my legs. I had no account of time, but then bright light broke through. My eyes remained shut. I felt hands on me, pulling me from the depths of my hiding place. Father held me close to him. *Are you okay, Ameera?*

I nodded with uncertainty. Something felt terribly wrong.

I remember: Aunty Rashida seated at the kitchen table, speaking to Mother. Other neighbours standing together and Uncle Yacoob busy on his phone. Mother lunged off her chair, when she noticed me, her arms outstretched, watery eyes focused on my face. Aunty Rashida reached for Mother and beckoned for her to sit down.

'Slowly, take it easy, Apa...'

Aunty Rashida was watching my face, waiting for me to say something. I was still looking at her when I felt Mother's hand in mine, her thumb gently rubbing my skin.

'Mummy, what's going on?' I asked.

Aunty Rashida motioned for me to sit down at the kitchen table, which I did. She sat opposite me. Uncle Yacoob had put away his cellphone.

Aunty Rashida was speaking to me, her soft, comforting manner contradicting the words coming from her mouth. 'Ameera, Anver met with an accident last night...'

'Where's he?' I thought I'd cried out, but it was more like a whisper. I looked from Mother, to Father, in search of you. Mother's cries pierced the silence.

***

I am so deep in thought that the clock chiming startles me. Does the pendulum still sway? I move away from the room and collect my belongings from the hallway. I pull open the heavy oak front door and step into the bright sunlight. The sudden light stings my tear-stained face. I pull the door closed, lock it, then throw the keys in through an open window. The estate agent can retrieve the keys from the floor.

I remember: shards of the story unfolding through the years, Mother choking on her tears. She spoke of your addiction. She spoke of drugs. It was only much later that I realised the extent of my sin. Anver, I am so sorry for everything...

No More Worries

On that Monday, at 4am in July, in the informal settlement within the grounds of Lenasia's extension 9, the temperature had dropped to the negatives. It would become warmer later, when the winter sun chased away the icy winds. But negative numbers at 4am, with sunrise only three hours later, suggested that tough judgement awaited those who took sleep within corrugated iron cages. The burden of frozen cold conditions pressed down on all the inhabitants in this settlement – the aged, the young, babies, adults, and strayed animals, each of whom submerged in their individual form of being, paused in their slumber, shivering limbs, all bracing themselves for the offensive assault of the day's icy winds.

The informal settlement's only living being seemingly undaunted by the dropping temperatures was Suhail Mangel, a twenty-seven-year-old man who had flown into gold-laden South Africa from India two years prior. Ensnared as he was in a life not wanted, and being long removed from his humane conscience, he peered out into the darkness at the baby which lay within his reach. A shiver vibrated within him, totally unrelated to the weather. It was as if his full form, his intestines which lay tangled in his gut, his heart which rhythmically pumped blood through him, and his star-shaped birthmark which lay hidden in the folds of his left leg – his whole being – was about to surrender to the anger trapped within him.

He watched the baby as it sucked peacefully on the dark nipple of the woman whose naked flesh he could feel. Suhail hoisted himself onto the point of his right elbow and projected his body closer to them, to breathe in their musky smell. He reached for them, drawing them into him, wondering what it felt like to be a baby. So powerless and yet equally powerful. Did he not control their paths with his recent existence?

The woman, his lover, rolled over onto her back. 'Why do you look at us like that?'

Suhail listened intently to her. He enjoyed hearing her accent. South African by birth, of Tswana ancestry, Sarah had been born Kelebogile Sarah Molefe. She had changed her first name, favouring her middle name to make it easier for when she worked as a domestic worker and later as a cashier. He despised that she had done that. It was something that they often fought about. He had also escaped a country where colonialism had once ruled, but he was not about to succumb to those who dictated his future. Sarah was a large woman, with a motherly bosom. Her stature had drawn him to her, twelve months prior, this form which enveloped him.

Unwilling to speak, he floated his attention past Sarah and the sleeping baby, beyond the corrugated sheets that now screeched in the wind, to the memories of others, in India, whom he had left behind. There, in a hut, situated within a land of dried-out crops, his other children slept cushioned on either side of their grandmother. Without good cause, except for the hungry need for his own survival, he had long overlooked ways of returning to his roots. He returned to lying on his back and pulled the blanket to his chin. If it weren't so damn cold, he would have sat outside the shack. They owned a small plot of red sand, and the landscape in and around Lenasia emanated overpopulation, with areas of informal settlements sprouting up on every plot of empty land. Suhail regarded this density as a far cry from the land which sprawled abundantly in his youth.

He opened his eyes and stared up at the patterned grooves in the corrugated sheet which swayed in the wind like ripples on water. He sighed, uneasy in his surroundings. His present life was not what he had envisioned the first time he'd stepped onto the property: their 'own' private land, barren of vegetation, decorated with plastic bottles, old torn tyres, and red sand, barricaded from the other properties by a thin wire fence. Every time he swept away the red sand that collected in the shack's entrance, he yearned for the bleached soil of his childhood. And that was a bad thing. He closed his eyes. Wind flowed through the holes in the corrugated sheets, bringing with it slivers of frost. Suhail barely registered this. He was reminiscing about his life's tale: how he had, with his wife's dreams and effort, imagined, planned, tilled, sweltered over, and laboured their happily ever after into existence, only to be bludgeoned into oblivion by the powers that be. Suhail jerked off the blanket, wrapped it over Sarah, and decided that he really needed his wife, his children, and the land of his birth. He yearned for them. His yearning and desperate desire to return to his roots were, he knew, the least of his worries. He needed money. Suhail Mangel had still not reaped his worth from the City of Gold.

***

Sarah's coarse voice sliced into his thoughts.

'Fuck it's cold!'

'Go make me a mug of coffee, won't you please, sweetie,' he retorted.

'I was up with the baby all night while you slept, and now I must get up to make for you what?'

Determined to ignore her, Suhail sat upright in the bed and pulled down his jersey, tightening it around him. He then reached for his overalls from the floor beside the bed. He climbed into them and zipped up the front. As he leaned against the bed, considering his next move, uproarious laughter floated into the shack. Daily, he would awake from restless slumber, hauled by the same boisterous laugh. He was plagued to know who possessed the nerve to wake them in the wee hours of every morning. And then one day during one of the many fights they had had recently, Sarah had revealed that they had become a topic of discussion in the neighbourhood. She had used the word *Coolie!* She said that the neighbours had wanted to know why she lived with him, the coolie. *Why not live in Lenasia?* Sarah said that she couldn't explain that he had no money and that the Indian people in Lenasia would not allow her to rent from them.

He went to the edge of the room that, in style, was a typical corrugated iron shack – you could step in through the front door and out through the back door. But the small space with its oak bedroom suite, solar-powered fridge, and microwave oven, had little in common with typical informal settlement shacks. And very unlike Suhail's birth home, this place spoke of wealth and exclusivity.

He flipped the switch of the electric kettle and watched the plastic panel glow red. Their newborn had captured the beating of Sarah's heart, which had once been his. They still made love. But when the baby cried, she would turn away from him, and place the baby's hunger over her full breasts.

As he stood there, waiting for the gentle whistle of the kettle to break into an outpour of steam, he thought back to the first time that they had met. They had both been working in Lenasia, a sprawling township created for brown-skinned South Africans during the apartheid years. She had taken a cashier job at Shoprite, and he had been the packer all the female workers had yearned for, because in those days, he was charming and motivated to climb the proverbial ladder to a managerial position.

A customer had brought in a case of long-life milk which she said was expired. Sarah had been on duty in the returns department, and Suhail was called to check the expiry date of the other boxes stacked on the shelf. He and Sarah never did check the boxes, because not long after the customer had been refunded, they had taken a lunch break, sat on the pavement facing the car park, and talked for the full hour.

Suhail had been immediately taken by Sarah's difference – her short frame, large bosom. Her laughter, he would discover, erupted from within her like jelly, wobbly and sweet. She was six years his senior, and because he was so desperate for some tender loving care, he'd decided that Sarah in his life might guarantee him South African citizenship.

Standing on the ice-cold cement, thinking about that first meeting, Suhail now felt his heart churning a blend of affection and revulsion. He remembered staring into her plump face, thinking she had the most sumptuous full fleshy lips when she licked them between small bites of bread. She had placed her other hand over his. Her touch had excited him, as had her seduction. Suhail had limited experience with women beyond the matrimonial chamber, and so he had shifted around nervously.

'Do you enjoy working here?' he had asked.

She had played with the orange, patterned scarf wrapped on her head, which he decided made her appear confident and in control.

'Yes, the job is good.' Her eyes found his.

She had tucked in the loose pieces of the headscarf, gently pulled at the long rings that hung from her ears, and then veered in close to him. He could smell the sweet scent of cooldrink on her breath.

'I worked my way up, and now I earn a lot more than the other ladies.' She had waved her hands in the air with satisfaction. 'And I have money saved in my bank account. Yes, I have a bank account.' She smiled at him, and her veneer had glinted gold in the sunlight. 'I'm saving to study. To become a lawyer.'

As she spoke, her Tswana face, which seemed to Suhail to be significantly large and yet suggestively adorable, had reminded him of an actress on television. And in that instant, he had wanted to own her. He had found her passion to save money and her yearning to study endearing. It had reminded him of himself. His desire for her had eroded all rational thinking. He did not realise that her wanting to study might also mean that she would evolve into an emotionally needy, dependent woman.

Suhail spooned two heaped teaspoons of coffee into a mug which he took from the oak cupboard. He then poured sugar straight from the canister into his mug. Sarah despised any mixing of spoons, so Suhail was cautious. He took the mug in both hands and ventured out of the shack into the early morning cold. He sat down on a stool with his back leaning against the corrugated panel of the shack for support. His gaze glided from the steel frame that guarded the periphery of their plot and the black dustbin which stood there, to the field of dried, hunched-over sunflowers whose heads sank into the soil only ten metres away from him. This was where the sewerage water ran in furrows that led, as far as he could tell, everywhere.

During summer, the sunflowers drained the water, standing tall and striking, their disc florets delivering pollen to the hundreds of bees which zoomed in. Suhail had developed an abnormal abhorrence for the bees and their buzzing. He despised how they sourced and collected pollen to be transported to their queen, who lounged delightfully in her hive. They did not need to wait on her, and even on this icy July morning, he hoped that the bees, when they returned, would display a wild transformation into self-serving creatures. He prayed for this change in his reality, too.

He sipped the last drops of coffee, gingerly rose, then opened the oak door to his homestead and stepped back in. He needed to keep his troubled mind employed. Sarah had switched on the television set, her eyes on the screen. The baby lay attached to her breasts. The election campaign – the lies, the promises delivered, the chanting from fellow believers – enraged him. Why was there always corruption in government in countries such as Africa and India? He placed the mug into a round bath of soapy water. Their kitchen – its granite-topped breakfast nook where they ate breakfast on Sunday mornings, the rose-designed dinner set stacked neatly on the shelf of the oak cabinet, the sink with its sink mixer tap which offered no water – all felt like a sham, like a set created for a television show.

He moved the mug around in the bath of soapy water – the suds nestled in his palm – and a trace of shimmer remained after they disappeared. Yes, they most definitely needed to fit a plumbing system. He left the mug to soak and heaved himself onto the oak kitchen stool which stood beneath the table nook. He sat there, staring at the television, with his thoughts trailing elsewhere.

Sarah's voice shattered the silence. 'What did you do with the money that you earned yesterday?' Then she broke into an uproar. There were napkins to be bought for their baby. Did he not see that the milk was finished? What about bread? What would they eat for supper? It was high time that he went out to find a decent paying job. Being idle was not going to put food on the table.

Suhail stood up and nearly knocked over the stool – it rocked before it settled back on its four legs.

'Oh, be quiet!' he said. Noticing the electric kettle, he decided on another cup of coffee and flipped on the switch. Sarah was right, but he felt helpless to remedy the situation. Suhail Mangel, former favourite packer at Shoprite, had been promoted to junior manager, only to be fired from his position when the xenophobic attacks of 2019 erupted in South Africa. Suhail had not held a decent job since. He knew the reason. His mother was angry and had cursed him. The deeper the curse raged, the greater his fear of rejection grew, and Suhail knew he had to return to his roots to heal the wounds now oozing with pus.

He nudged at the woollen jersey he wore beneath his overalls. He had always disliked the bristly feel of wool on his bare skin. He was finally beginning to surrender to the morning temperature – and thought about opening the door, but if he did that, the baby would feel the cold. During these past weeks, Suhail had learnt how challenging it was to keep the room at perfect baby temperature.

He retrieved his used mug from the plastic wash basin, and using a clean dish towel, quickly dried it. While he prepared a fresh mug of coffee, he considered his plans for the day. As the warm liquid caressed his insides, he was aware that Sarah had just touched the soft flesh of the baby's cheek, angling his face to her other breast.

Sarah was also watching his every movement. 'You have got to get to the supermarket for nappies today, okay!' she said softly.

The gentle calm hung around them, gathering clouds before the raging storm.

'Yes, yes, I do, but there is no money left from yesterday,' he responded. The baby had unlatched and was now observing him with fascination. Suhail wanted to feel warm, confident, and in control, not envious and frustrated.

Everything got to Sarah Molefe, especially since the birth of the baby, when she was forced to stay at home. She rested her hand in her hair, pulling at the braids, twirling them around her fingers. For a woman, she had unusually large fingernails, and she had not for a while noticed that the pink nail polish was scraped off at the cuticles.

'Can you give me money?'

'Are you crazy?' she screamed. 'Why don't you push trolleys and collect garbage the way the other men do!'

'I don't want to do that job!'

She shook her head and clicked her tongue.

'There is money in your bank account.' Suhail traced the outlined pattern on the mug he held.

'Yes, there is, but you can't bloody touch that.' She pulled at her braids again. 'The issue is...' She adjusted the coils of braids, tugging them together into a ponytail. When had her hair become so spirally and wild? 'That I can't possibly get to the bank in this state.'

This was a tough situation. No anger now. Her black eyes softened, and her face revealed genuine distress. Suhail sighed, realising the Catch-22 of their situation. He needed Sarah as much as she needed him. For now, anyway.

'Okay, surely I can withdraw some cash using your ATM card.'

'I have a limit on my card.' The coolness was back. 'You will only be allowed an allowance of R500.'

Suhail felt the blood running through a vein on his forehead thicken with throbbing beats. His left ear grew hot, and the heat spread through him. The witch! 'Well then, R500 it is. I will withdraw the money and—'

'Return the card to me,' she snapped. 'I can always cancel future transactions.'

'I need permission from the lady of the house, beautiful madam. Mother of my child' – he winked – 'you control the purse strings.'

Annoyed, Sarah handed over the card. 'I don't want you pulling that shit on me, Suhail, you hear. You get the money, buy the napkins, bread, milk, and two Chicken Licken lunch meals. That's it. You walk back home. You will not use my money to pay for a taxi.'

An urge to swear at Sarah surged through him, but Suhail rarely lost his outward calm. Only beneath, in the profound stowage of his mind, did he bellow and shout profanities. He delivered his used mug to the bowl, then went into the corner of the room (where he kept his clothes in a tall oak cupboard) and grabbed socks, a clean white shirt and black jeans. He dressed quickly. He fished out his backpack – the one he used when going out – from under the bed. He opened the bag's middle compartment and put the card safely into a hidden zipped pocket. *Let's do this.*

'Relax my love.' And with that, he pulled open the heavy oak door and headed into the icy gust of wind. Suhail could feel Sarah's gaze on him, following him.

Suhail exited the house and stepped onto the barren earth of their yard. He passed the black plastic bin, totally missing it, and stared into the distance, searching through the dense fog for the road. A stray dog ventured near, smelling of sewage – its coat hung thinly over his ribbed frame. Suhail took in its stench and decided this was a bad day, despite his having something to do – an errand to run to make his existence seem useful. He withdrew a balaclava from his backpack, and pulled it over his face, masking it all – head, face, and neck – from the full measure of the cold. Could he be lucky enough to catch a taxi to Signet Terrace shopping centre at this time of the morning? Then he remembered that he had no money. He gazed at the wild weeds flooring the dry red earth where he stood: chunks of frost and melted water shied behind rocks and between crevices. He looked to the sky in search of the rising sun. Nothing.

He moved towards the diamond-pattern mesh fencing and gate that had been crafted to keep out animals. Holes where the barrier had been pulled apart allowed stray animals to seek refuge in their yard. The fencing was locked with a padlock and chain.

The lock would not budge. The key did not turn. Not at all. The frost and rust were a lock sealer. 'Fuck!' he cried, flinging up his arms. How many people on this earth dealt with early morning negativities? How did they convert them to good energies? He banged at the lock, smashing the key in and out, in and out.

Suhail placed his hands on the gate, which was covered in

an uneven layer of ice. He pulled at the top bars of the gate, and without realising it, plastered his hands into the ice. As he tried to get his hands free, fragments of skin tore away, and pain spiralled up from the soles of his feet to the tips of his hair. He lost his balance and collapsed on the wet earth. Had he just been struck by lightning? Impossible. There were no clouds beyond the mist. Suhail turned again to the fence, struggling to stand. His feet remained anchored in the soil. Strong roots rose, twined and bound his feet. He reached down to pull them away. He saw nothing. The sharp sensation of ropes slicing into his skin remained. Fear submerged him. He rose first to all fours, dog-like and barking. He stood up, held firmly to the gate, inserted the key in once more, this time slowly, and he turned it, pleading – second by second – knowing that Allah could still hear him.

***

By the time Suhail had opened the gate, the sun had risen an inch into the sky, and he realised Sarah was no longer watching him. Witch! Suhail's resentment masked his panic. She hadn't even the humanity to rescue him. He had no idea what had happened there on the damp ground by the gate. It must have been his imagination. He left the gate open with the lock hanging on its chain. Once he was within a kilometre of the road, he caught a whiff of the stink. They lived illegally on land that did not have municipal garbage collection. Instead of hauling their trash to the landfill site, the residents had decided the best thing to do was to accumulate the waste on a piece of empty land at the edge of the settlement. He eyed the fermenting heap with disgust and fastened his balaclava over his face.

A real fuckup – both his life and the dumping issue. Suhail worked hard to focus on the positive. He had a roof over his head, even though he felt these days as though he slept with the enemy. He was thankful that she had at least given him her debit card and PIN. And by the time he was done getting the nappies and other goods, maybe, after doing the errands, he would find the courage to use some of the money, buy a pack of cigarettes, take himself to a park and relax. He turned out of the settlement, onto the main road out of Extension 9, to Lenasia. Here the 'trolley men' had congregated on the road in front of the road sign to Extension 9, and they leaned over their trolleys, dressing them in coarse, hay-coloured sacks. Suhail did not want to converse with them. He wanted to turn around and return to his shack, but the men were deeply involved in their job and did not look his way. He hurried on, his walk shifting into a jog, and he ran on, past the building which read 'Casa Mia', past flats, houses, Trade Route Mall, and onto Nirvana Drive into Lenasia. He hiked west on Nirvana Drive. Five kilometres or so from the turn-off to Extension 9, the road became a thick, three-lane braid. If you followed it far enough, it intersected with the railway lines where one would find actual trains and a train station. He passed a cyclist, who was riding too slowly, and fished in his pocket for a cigarette. Nothing. Not even a stick of chewing gum. Why hadn't he brought something to eat? Suhail shook his head and tried not to care. His stomach growled. He took a left turn onto Protea Avenue, passing the three bakeries, where an aroma swirl of hot, oven-baked breads assaulted his senses. The distinctive composition of barking dogs, mewling cats, and roaring vehicles rose from the surrounds. He thought he detected the low rumble of distant thunder. His feet, dressed in tekkies, hurriedly crunched and punched the stones between large bricks.

On his way to Signet Terrace, Suhail allowed his mind to wander off dreamily. In his daydream, he had accrued money, lots of it, and used it to return home. His children welcomed him with outstretched arms. His mother looked on happily, while his wife, dressed in a red panjabi, offered him a tray laden with sweetmeats.

Brightly coloured large pictures of bowls of curry on a red face-brick wall summoned him back to harsh reality. His stomach growled with hunger.

As he passed through the fence alongside the boom gates, a guard who appeared to be in his twenties, with short black hair hidden under a red beret, leaned on the side of the boom gate and growled, 'Wait outside! We open in ten minutes!'

Suhail wanted to punch that sneer right off his face; he wanted the steel rod of the boom gate to become unstable and fall on top of him. *Young man, even if you think that you are some EFF hero, you can lose your job within a second, and then I will laugh... So just quit the arrogance.* Suhail wanted to say that, but felt satisfied thinking it. Instead, he pretended to send a message on his battery-dead phone. His gaze settled on a thin older woman speaking to a tall older man with deep wrinkles ridging on his face.

The woman cast a sideway glance at Suhail that was part shock, part worry, and said, 'Monna o wa re utlwa.' She hurried her partner through the open gate.

In one hand she clutched a torn green identity book, and in the other a large, leather-bound handbag.

Suhail removed his balaclava, pulled his bag to the front, and opened the zipper, then tried to push in the balaclava. Something cold jabbed at his hand, and he dropped the bag to the ground, unzipped the compartment, and rummaged in with both hands to see what he had found. There, hidden beneath a jacket, Suhail saw a toy gun. Sarah must have purchased it. She had revealed to him once that she was afraid of the neighbours since they questioned her living with him. He left the gun hidden beneath the jacket, closed the bag, and swung it over his shoulder. He turned on the balls of his feet and went through the gates.

As he strode through the bitter cold, feeling mysteriously more assertive, he surveyed the scene. Mr EFF stood at the boom gate, manually opening and closing for cars to enter. The couple had disappeared, and as he scanned the centre in search of them, he glimpsed them entering Standard Bank. Seven or eight people were standing around outside Wimpy, possibly waiting for the Eldos bus to collect them. A woman sifting through the trash in the dirt bins stopped when she realised that she was being watched. In his mind, he dared her to say one cheeky word. He continued to the bank, grateful that the centre was quiet. When he neared his destination, he wrenched off his jacket. Never mind the cold. The wind felt good. The bag fell with a thud to the floor.

Inside the bank, a long line of people waited to withdraw and deposit large sums of cash. If you withdrew less than R2000, the ATM was where you went. He slammed the card into the machine, punched in the PIN, and waited. He grabbed the wads of cash and shoved them, with the ATM card, into the zipped compartment of his bag. Suhail closed the short distance to Chicken Licken to place the order.

'Brrr. It's cold, isn't it,' the cashier said.

'Yes, yes, it is,' Suhail said.

The cashier had large breasts. He liked large breasts, but he had come here on a mission. He looked up at the menu with its orange-tainted photos of delicious food. In all honesty, he could survive his hunger pangs. This was his chore, his job. He could do it. Slavery without protest – that needed to be his new dictum – until the day Sarah fully trusted him.

'Can I please order two Chicken Licken lunch meals, thank you.' He needed to get the food, the napkins, and return home soon.

'Okay, that will be R99,80.' She tipped the visor of her black hat to acknowledge his order. 'Will you be having anything else with that?' She clicked her tongue. Ugly teeth. There were gaps, probably knocked out in a brawl.

'No thanks.' He felt himself scowl. He couldn't help himself.

He was beginning to realise the full value of *his* Sarah. He was happy that he had accepted her request for him to do the shopping. If Sarah could not cope physically, he would be there to assist her. Sarah was prized, he thought, pausing to watch the cashier at the till, taking note of how she flicked at her nose using her forefinger. He needed Sarah for her beauty, her delicious cooking, being the mother to their child. Not her money. Shit. He lifted his bag and swung it onto his back – Sarah didn't trust him anymore.

Soon after he had lost his job at Shoprite, the uncle of his childhood friend had offered him a job in his fruit-and-veg shop. The salary would have been minimal, but he would have received tips from the customers when he carried their shopping bags to the car. Suhail had been told the rags-to-riches tale of

Uncle Abdul Hamid, who now owned multiple blocks of flats on one road, and he was eager to know the trade secrets behind this Indian uncle. Suhail had accepted the job but had then left when he was told that Uncle Abdul Hamid would never allow Sarah to live with him. Sarah had been upset that he hadn't told her, and she had found out from a friend. She had refused to believe that he had left the job for her. On that day, between sobs, she had told him that she had expected so much more from him... and he had disappointed her. Recalling these events, Suhail felt the need to hold her. He would win back her trust.

Suhail turned around. The cashier paused before entering the kitchen.

'How long will the order take to make?' His voice echoed across the silent parking lot.

'Fifteen minutes,' she said.

He nodded. 'I will return to collect,' he called over his shoulder, as he stepped into the winter sun.

His hopefulness mingled with the cold breeze and gave Suhail the motivation he sought. It took him all of fifteen minutes to happily gallivant in Shoprite's aisles to get the much-needed items.

His colleagues at Shoprite shied away from him. He knew they pitied him. Their reproach hurt him. His earlier anger rose again. There was no place for him anywhere. Laden with groceries and soaking in the delicious aroma of the Chicken Licken, he strode to the exit gates.

Suhail took a left onto Guinea Fowl Street, which meant that he was heading back to Extension 9. He checked the time on his cellphone and then swore because he had forgotten that its battery had gone flat. It couldn't be past ten. He was sure that Sarah was in bed with their baby, probably sleeping or suckling the infant.

He watched the men at Mica, dressed in overalls and busily carrying wood and paint tins to a truck. The driver pulled on a cigarette, heaving out plumes of smoke. *Hell, I've come this far, I might as well relish a smoke.* With quickened strides, while keeping watch for a security guard, Suhail made his way to the parked white Hilux bakkie. The labourers, their attention distracted, continued their jobs. The buyers bought. The managers yelled out instructions. Suhail leaned his elbow on the rim of the opened window. A lizard with greenish scales scuttled from its resting place on top of a brick into the crevices between them. Suhail barely noticed the flick of this movement.

'Salaam. Howzit? Do you have an extra smoke?'

The driver pulled a cigarette from the pack and passed one to him. Suhail cupped the beast in his hands, rolling it between his palms, and then placed the cigarette between his lips. The man lit it, and Suhail inhaled, allowing the smoke to soothe his soul.

As he stood there, trying to redeem his thoughts, and having just surrendered to a drug while still clinging onto the window of the van, he staggered through what had just glazed over his awareness. He had to return to his roots. Amid his frustration, Suhail tried to untangle the thoughts that lay knotted within him: his family in India whom he had promised to return to, the xenophobic attacks, the retrenchment letter, refusing the job at Uncle Abdul Hamid's shop, the shack of rich oak, Sarah, their baby, and now the intense desire to escape everything. He pressed his head into his hands and tried to solve the puzzle. And then with his open palm, he pushed away from the van, withdrawing. Suhail watched the driver, who had been staring at him from his seat, lean his head out of the window. Suhail tried to grab the man's outstretched hand, willing for help in unveiling the trauma within.

Suhail, urgency tugging at his bones, went through the opened gates, making sure he stayed on his route. He wound his way back towards Nirvana Drive, trying to make sense of himself, those lasting realities that led only to insecurities threatening to noose his existence.

A sorrow as heavy as the dense morning mist engulfed him.

***

Ahead, the couple he had seen earlier were walking his path. He struggled against slowing down and kept up his pace, knowing he would pass them soon enough. As the distance between them grew smaller, the road looked much quieter now that he was entering the residential areas with the streets forking this way and that. Suhail sped up – Sarah would be waiting. Despite his attempt at positivity, his anguish consumed him. Here he was, alone in this foreign country, without work and money, and living with a woman who doubted him. How much worse could life get?

'Fuck!' he shouted.

As he drew nearer to the couple, he could make out their words. He understood some of them, even though they spoke Setswana.

'Did you put the money away properly?' the tall man asked.

'Yes, I did. It's here.' She patted the bag. 'Inside.' She smiled at him. 'Just think, Charlie. Now we can buy a fridge and a mattress.'

Suhail knew what he had to do but wasn't sure if he could. He reached into his bag. Carrying the gun felt like a sin; holding it felt like a noose around his neck. He looked into the cloudy sky, whispered, 'Please forgive me.' Suhail tried not to feel. He did not want a single emotion to journey through him. In the thick, thin and brawny spaces of his hand – in every microscopic cell – he poked the gun into the woman's ribs and jabbed deeper. Her screams ravaged him.

And then he saw them. He saw them in the woman's widened eyes. He heard them in the deafening screams of the older man. Suhail's mother and the hungry faces of his children rose around him. He cried out. He thrashed his arms at them, to ward them off.

'Please forgive me! Please forgive me!' he pleaded.

He dropped the gun. He fell to his knees. He put his hands together.

'Please forgive me!'

It was then that he felt the old woman's hand on his head. He looked up. He saw his own mother.

'May you be granted peace from your pain,' she whispered.

Suhail felt a sudden release of tension. He was reaching through a fracture in life's eclectic frame, making contact with the spiritual sphere. He wanted to believe that his mother had come to rescue him from this life, but that would not be.

He was now a husband and a father. A second time around. A second chance to make it work. Sarah had always pleaded for a life with no worries.

He would give her that life.

The Ungrateful Daughter-in-law

Charmaine awoke from her own dreams of desire. One handsome man with protruding chest muscles and a loincloth swooned around her. Her rational, living mind intruded: the scene was all wrong, the man, with his long, curly hair, was not her own Iqbal. With his full mane of hair, he resembled the hero on the front cover of the historical romance she kept hidden in her underwear drawer. Or was he somebody else?

A detached thought returned, one that Charmaine seldom allowed to form in her mind – *Iqbal did not feature in her dreams*.

She was awake, that much she knew; it was four o'clock in the morning. The four-legged walker creaked on the wooden floor as her mother-in-law entered the bathroom. On either side of Charmaine, two girl children breathed deeply, dummies plugged into their mouths while they slept peacefully, oblivious to their mother's rhythmic movements. Another human, probably the helper, entered the bathroom, muttering intensely and issuing instructions in jovial tones, or so it seemed to Charmaine, who was still floating in her dreamy, intoxicated state.

Finally, her mother-in-law, followed by the helper, exited the bathroom. The helper stepped away from the older lady to reveal a body naked from the waist down. Her mother-in-law insisted on being dressed in the paak confines of her own room. She was obsessive about cleanliness. Yes, but surely the helper could cover the older woman and not rob her of her dignity? The helper turned and looked at Charmaine, who pretended to be asleep.

The helper returned to the bathroom to clean up. Iqbal's soft mumbles became audible, from somewhere close to the kitchen. The messy bathroom had been washed clean, all sterile and fresh in its stark whiteness. Ready, Charmaine thought, for her twin daughters to wreck the place with toothpaste and shampoo suds. Somewhere, the radio was switched on, and the loud, melodious voice of Zain Bhika filtered through the house.

Suddenly, Charmaine had an agonising need to make ghusl, to wash the sin from her body. Thoughts from her dream returned, the large-muscled man teasing her with an adoration she could only concoct in her mind, because she had never, in her own reality, experienced such love. She dismissed the thoughts she was creating; she felt more desire for a character from her book than she did for her own husband.

Where had Iqbal slept last night? But compelled by the persistent need to cleanse herself before performing the early morning prayer, she lazily followed the trail of her thoughts. Her mother-in-law must have warmed his food when he returned late last night from his weekly zikr recitals. An emotional and immensely loving human, her mother-in-law would have made sure that her son had his fill of food and saw to it that his body lay warm beneath the covers. But she, her mother-in-law, his mother, must stop treating Iqbal as a prince to be worshipped – an error which was sure to result in grave consequences

She was shuffling to the bathroom when she remembered that she was wearing only skimpy underwear. Iqbal liked to feel her beside him as he fell asleep.

Without her spectacles, she couldn't locate her black satin gown anywhere. Anyway, she would be removing all her clothing to shower, so it didn't matter that her flesh was on display when she entered the bathroom. She rushed there.

'Er, excuse me Charmaine, we forgot Ouma's hair band on the sink. I just came to get it.'

She turned to find the helper, Aunty Nelly, standing in the doorway. A bemused look painted her face.

'Haai, Nelly, don't you know how to knock?' she asked from behind the bathroom door.

'We have the same hanging things, eh sisi.' Nelly giggled. 'What's there to hide?'

Charmaine liked the woman instinctively, and she felt happy

somehow, calm and content, totally within her being.

'And we both need to lose all this tummy fat,' she said, more to herself. Again, the handsome man's face intruded, floating in her mind's eye. The handsome man, ready with love, only to realise that his maiden was large around the waist. Going through his thoughts would be pointless. He was, after all, a figment of her imagination, and he would love her no matter the size of her protruding belly. Iqbal was, of course, another matter. She remembered his hostile brashness on their wedding night when he had to prove her virginity. He was the only son caring for his widowed mother and could not find a willing bride, and even when he did, he had no money to give the girl his best. Perhaps he had settled for her because she wore a similar brand, and anyway, a woman to give him children and see to his desires and needs was better than no woman at all.

But she also remembered the humble warmth in his manner to her. He had offered to help her in the kitchen, and did the laundry; with instinctive knowing grace of a protective husband, he saw to it that she was well fed and happy throughout the nine months of her pregnancy. She must have been insufferable back then, angry, and oppressive, because she could think of nothing but her anguish, the tortured pain she wore in her broken heart, after being denied her first love.

'Sometimes, I think that I should have married Iqbal,' Rabia had said, offering this confession on a warm midsummer night as she played with the loose end of her scarf.

'He loved me, you know, and I denied him.' This was the first time she had ever said something directly. She was Iqbal's cousin, his khala's daughter. He loved her loudness, her brash, boisterous laugh, as animated as Nelly's. He had wooed and humoured her, and she made Charmaine jealous. The sensual splendour of her voice, the warm laughter that consumed the house – she had a gift for expression, for telling a tale that made her impossible to ignore. It made one look childish not to be joyful in the way she celebrated living.

Did Iqbal know how much Charmaine disliked the woman? What would he do if Rabia asked to be with him, with them? Would he marry her, take her on as a second wife? Yes, he might,

Charmaine said to herself. Yes, it was something he would do with full knowledge that it was within his Islamic right to wed more than one.

She turned on the water and stood under the shower; she enjoyed the water caressing her skin. It was one of the simple pleasures of life, the gift of being able to be cleansed fully, with the flow of hot water. She was grateful. She begged forgiveness for her sins and felt satisfied with the belief that she had been pardoned.

She would recompense, as she served him his tea, for denying him her love, for the cruel manipulation of her position as the mother of his children. How things had changed. In the old days, he would have taken her without considering her pain. Verses quoted from the religious scriptures told that the angels cursed a woman who denied her husband's needs. Clothing roughly pulled away, popping buttons – beware the sacred husband and his desires, conquering the body which was his to control. No need for all that now, this new era where women are courageous enough to take their husbands to task for marital abuse.

She rehearsed how she would say sorry; she would wake early and prepare a morning meal for everybody – fresh round rotis and masala-fried scrambled eggs. First, she would serve her mother-in-law and then she would loudly exclaim, 'Praise be to Allah, Mummy, I am so blessed for you and Iqbal!'

Her mother-in-law would smile and say, 'Iqbal, I told you that you married a gem,' and he would smile, and Charmaine would feel all exalted and dignified.

In her cupboard, she found new, clean blue jeans and a long-sleeved, peach-coloured blouse. Iqbal was calling to tell her that breakfast was ready. What did her mother-in-law think of her, daughters-in-law like her, the new breed who led their own lives?

Her mother-in-law held an aged face with sharp wrinkles running grooves into her face. Mid-seventies, old enough to remember her own mother as a daughter-in-law and old enough to have lived through it herself. Obliging young girl, angry father-in-law who screamed at her and cursed her every time she served tea a few minutes late because it took longer than expected to bath and present herself in her new bride finery. She was promised the gift of paradise for her patience and obedience, while her husband was promised seventy-two virgins in paradise, all with splendid beauty. Ah, the irony of it all.

Out in the passage, a small breather before beginning the day, her mother-in-law was standing at the kitchen counter. She was kneading the dough into a smooth ball before she rolled it in swift movements into round rotis. Under the counter, her body leaned on the walker in an approach of complete dependency. A long green dress gave her waist an aged stockiness. Charmaine stood at the entrance, observing her mother-in-law's swiftness. Then she pulled a chair from under the round table and settled down into it. Sweat shimmered on the older woman's face, and Charmaine watched how she wiped it away with the back of her hand, wiped her nose in the same movement, and then continued with the rotis. The soiled hand, evidence of her disregard of cleanliness, stayed with Charmaine, even though she tried to dismiss the thought by reprimanding herself soundlessly for this repulsion. Still, it would be wonderful if the older woman washed her hands after dealing with the sweat, even if she merely wiped her hands on a dishcloth and then washed it later. Anything would be better than that disregard of cleanliness, the chance encounters with those who see. But the older woman's disregard was a part of the indifference with which she wore her life.

She was her mother-in-law, she was every woman whom she had ever known and whose toil remained governed, and sanctioned by the men who controlled her living. Even her own mother, who had birthed and suckled her, whom she had admired and idolised for her culinary and home-making skills, had taken on a role as submissive helper responsible for the daily chores of their home. And for her mother's protest, ah, the stark awakening that the threat of divorce brought at once to their peaceful charade.

'Charmaine? Is everything okay?' Iqbal intruded on her reflection. *What is wrong with me? Why did I marry in the first place when I knew that this was not the life I wanted?*

'I'm not okay,' she said, her manner rattled.

'Oh, my love, what's wrong?' he asked her. 'Go lie down. I will bring your breakfast to bed.'

'The girls have their immunisation today,' her mother-in-law said.

'I will take them, Ma. Can you please come with to help settle them?' her husband asked.

Her mother-in-law glanced her way, placed the plate with the piled rotis on the table, in front of her son, then pulled a chair out and sat down.

Charmaine left them and climbed into bed. Things had changed. Now homes included daughters-in-law like her, liberated and obstinate, leading contemporary lives like women anywhere in the world. But thirty-odd years ago, she would have been one of the few daughters-in-law dressed in jeans, joining her husband at the table to eat her mother-in-law's cooked food, after hours of sleeping or whatever it was that had kept her so busy. In every other house there would have been beautifully dressed daughters-in-law serving hot food to their husbands and in-laws – pleasant daughters-in-law, submissive daughters-in-law, keeping the children quiet while the elders ate. Then they, the daughters-in-law, would clean away the dishes and pack away the food, and only then would they sit in the kitchen to eat the leftovers. Before seeing to their husband's needs, they would first rub their mother-in-laws' feet and sit with them while they discussed the next day's menu. At the crack of dawn, they would rush out into the yard to collect the eggs from the hen, and another fat hen to be plucked, cleaned, and washed. After serving a breakfast of fried eggs and polony to all and sundry, another day of cleaning garlic or ginger or grinding dhana jeeroo would unfold.

'Those days we had barkhat in time,' they said. There was always plenty of time.

On impulse, she pulled out an e-cigarette from the drawer next to her bed, hidden beneath piles of lacy underwear. An old album fell out with the clothing piled on top. Even when she had drawn in a long drag of the vape, she continued to suck on it, allowing her thoughts to sprawl out. She opened the album and began paging through it, pictures from her wedding day, pictures of university days and school, pictures of the Simply Food restaurant her father had once owned, where she and Jake had shared a secret place hidden behind the shelves of sauces. In those days, the restaurant had a kind of crazy liveliness, teenagers braving their parents, hanging out, often helping with the washing up to pay for their meal. Life in Father's Simply Food had been bizarrely dynamic then, given that her relationship with Jake had been a big secret. Now the place was quiet in an eerie sort of way, with hungover old people hanging onto each other, in search of a healing meal, and beggars hogging the entrance, in search of free food.

Jake was gone, had moved with his mother to the Free State, or wherever it was that they took white boys to keep them away from dark-skinned girls they claimed to love. There had been no whites in Lenasia then. He had come to train Father how to run the franchise, and he had stayed, but his presence had been like the glare of light reflected off a window. And the afterthought of him remained like a darkened smudge that the bright light marked on your vision. The discovery of their relationship was inevitable, and when the shit had hit the fan, he left.

'I am going to speak to your dad today, to ask for your hand in marriage,' he had said. Then he had nuzzled his face into her hair.

'When will you tell your parents?' she had asked.

'Tonight,' he had said.

Charmaine realised the emotional reason she was paging through the photo album, and scolded herself out loud, 'Come on, Charmaine! You are now a married woman!' Her husband was bringing her breakfast in bed. Awake now, the twins were giggling together and would be overjoyed that their father would take them to the doctor. Happiness made them overexcited. She could see them dressed in their Sunday best – sitting in the backseat of the car, wriggling out of tied seat belts, jumping all over.

She opened the drawer and hid the album, deep under her nightclothes and lingerie, in the back corner.

Iqbal was at the door, balancing a tray of breakfast delicacies in his outstretched hands. He registered Charmaine's startled look, placed the tray onto the dressing table, and held out a mug of tea, which she accepted.

He pounced on the twins like a huge grizzly growling bear, and they hid under the duvet, giggling and screaming. He laughed and hugged them.

'How are my twinkle twins?'

'We also want breakfast in bed!' they screamed in chorus.

'Shoo, poppies, Mummy is not feeling too well today. Go have your breakfast in the kitchen. Daadi has hot sugar roti for you. Then we are going out.'

The twins climbed off the bed and hurried from the room.

Iqbal placed the tray on Charmaine's lap. He looked into the already unreadable depths of Charmaine's eyes, as if envisaging questioning the lies she had just told – 'Why did you tell a lie? You are not sick' – but he didn't speak his mind; he turned away and left the room, no doubt creating a story to tell his mother.

When they had left for the doctor's, and after a long, luxurious soak in a bath laced with bath oils, Charmaine politely accepted words of comfort from Aunty Nelly – Iqbal had informed the helper of her current display of illness. Charmaine's very presence as mother to the twins, and daughter-in-law living with a mother-in-law 'while being ill', only fortified the labour of her endurance.

Promptly after her bath, she called her father to tell him that she was not well and would not be visiting him on the weekend, as planned. No, no, she had not been to the doctor's but would go right away.

Then, just as she settled into bed with the television remote, the picture on the screen zoned out, and the house became silent. Someone somewhere sitting in a raised chair of control at City Power had switched off the electricity and booted Lenasia into four hours of load shedding. She tossed the remote. 'Why didn't anybody tell me?' So now the house – the washing machine, that contraption that should purify the clothing, as her mother-in-law always said with sarcasm – was lying clogged with murky water. Clothing had to be removed and hung, dishes piled onto basin tops unwashed, a vacuum cleaner gone silent. 'And my phone battery is on its last two percent!' she ranted.

She stood at the glass door, staring out over the gigantic grey machine that was the generator. Pull out the generator, pull out the choke, switch it on or – switch it on and then pull out the choke, was that what Iqbal had said? She didn't know the process – how to switch on the generator. She couldn't remember. Aunty Nelly stood beyond the gate, watching her. Anyway, Aunty Nelly had already placed the clothing in a large enamel bath outside on the grass and picked up what seemed to be the stick of a broom, probably to toss the clothing around in the same fashion as a washing machine. Perhaps the clothes washed cleaner this way. She didn't know and didn't wait around to see.

Usually, she had to make an effort to remind herself of her place as Iqbal's wife. Not many daughters-in-law in the modern living system chose to live with in-laws; it depended not only on your husband's finances but also on the role he played within the family – his emotional worth. This morning, she suffered inner irritation with the course that her life had taken.

Iqbal had accepted her tale of being ill without battle. He had acknowledged her complaints with concern. Was his concern a pretence, was he playing her game, or had he finally abandoned her to her own devices?

She went over the events leading to their matrimony in her mind. Her power of refusal was at its greatest. She had fought off her father, who had wanted her to stay with him, to not marry another. She would be sacrificing too much of herself, she had explained. Her father had been taken aback by her outcry; it dissolved all the fight in his being.

Aunty Nelly resumed her stirring of the clothes with the wooden broom. The gush of water, its shivering cold, had summoned a hidden detail from the day before her nikaah. Charmaine shut her eyes and remembered her aunts cleansing bloody chickens of their dirt in cold water, in preparation for the wedding biryani. And her father's voice rose among others. So isolated and yet distinct. Was life not a test, he had asked. They all agreed, chanting in unison. And God tested only his favoured servants and blessed them for their sacrifice with gifts in this world and the next. Father whispering, Father praying,

Father pleading like he did with her mother, the day that she had walked out, leaving him with a three-year-old daughter to mother. He was a living example of God's favour, he had boasted.

Yes, God gave you only that which you could deal with.

If Father had not been present that day to carry away the plastic baths of washed chicken pieces, she knew she would not have consented to her nikaah. She had given in. She was the victim of her fate. Everybody had been made to know. Charmaine was not one to keep her suffering silent.

'It was all a charade, but unto what end?' she said to the empty room.

Speaking the unspeakable out loud had evoked pity from people. Outsiders unapologetically chastised her for being rude. Had he not saved her, they rebuked. She should be thankful that she married into a good home. Was she not the haraami who had loved a non-Muslim boy, they gossiped. They spat the words out with venomous distaste.

Another painful memory intruded. She had feasted ravenously on her love with Jake, until the day her father discovered it and then it was suddenly something she had to live down.

'Charmaine, please don't...'

'I love him, Daddy! Don't you see that?'

'Don't leave me. Don't leave me for Jake.'

'I would never leave you, Daddy! Why do you think that?'

'Because it is what your mother did...'

She remembered her father's words in every aspect, and his sadness, acknowledged his suspicions about her, about who she was – as her mother's child.

Her heart ached. She needed to halt the flow of thoughts. She retreated to her room and swallowed a few painkillers for the headache that now overwhelmed her. She packed away her memories. She would rest, and when Iqbal returned with the twins, she would be healed – healed until her memories threatened again, to eat away her being.

Acknowledgements

Producing this collection has been long and arduous but also an extremely enriching experience. To my publisher, Colleen Higgs and the team at Modjaji Books, thank you for all your support in getting this collection to the point of perfection. A huge thank you to Helen Moffett for her careful and insightful reading. I am so grateful to you. Thank you to Nerine Dorman for the initial edits and valued recommendations. Thank you to Jesse Breytenbach for designing a deep and symbolic cover. Thank you to Nedine Moonsamy for penning the foreword. I appreciate the time that friends took to read the book and to provide valuable feedback. Finally, I am grateful for the love and continued support from my husband, Suleiman. Thank you is not enough.

About the Author

Zaheera Jina Asvat has been described as a writer and an academic. She holds a PhD in mathematics education from WITS University, South Africa and is a lecturer at the Wits School of Education. Zaheera is the author of *Surprise!* and the StimuMath programme for pre-schoolers. She is the editor of *Tween Tales 1*, *Tween Tales 2*, *Saffron* and *Riding the Samoosa Express*. In addition, Zaheera is the curator of Jozi's Books and Blogs Festival, a non-profit initiative aimed at inspiring expression through reading, writing and the arts in the less-affluent areas of Gauteng. Zaheera lives in Lenasia, South Africa with her husband, three sons, and many in-laws.

Printed in the United States
by Baker & Taylor Publisher Services